NUM NOMS™

Smell so delicious!

Collector's Guide

PaRragon

Bath · New York · Cologne · Melbourne · Delhi
Hong Kong · Shenzhen · Singapore

This Book Belongs to

This edition published by Parragon Books Ltd in 2017 and distributed by

Parragon Inc.
440 Park Avenue South, 13th Floor
New York, NY 10016
www.parragon.com

Written and designed by Rich T Media Ltd. for Parragon Books Ltd.

ISBN 978-1-4748-3398-1

Printed in China

NUM NOMS™
Smell so delicious!™

Welcome!

Have you caught the Num Noms collecting craze yet? There are lots of flavorful families including Jelly Bean, Cupcake, Ice Cream, and many more. These oh-so-cute mini food dishes smell delicious, too. There's Nilla Swirl with her fresh vanilla scent, the birthday cake aroma of Suzy Stripes, and Tropi-Cali Pop's dream mango fragrance. From strawberry and chocolate ice cream to fries and ketchup, it's a scent-sational world that you have to explore!

The egg-citing news is you can combine these mini food dishes to make your own refreshing recipes. Place a Nom at the bottom and stack one or more Nums on top. Create a banana split ice cream by putting Choco Cream and Billy Banana on top of Mintee Gloss-Up. Or head to the diner and try Hammy Burger and Frenchie Fries on top of Ketchup Go-Go. Build tasty towers or silly stacks . . . it's a piece of cake!

With hundreds of Num Noms to collect, there's an endless number of combos you can try. But with so many sweet 'n' savory lovelies, it's berry hard to keep track of them. That's why we've squeezed all of them inside the Num Noms Collector's Guide. Ready to taco 'bout the cuties some more? Turn the page to get started. . . .

Total Treats

Inside this cool Collector's Guide, every single Num Nom is waiting to say hello to you!

For starters, you'll find the **Nums**. These **lovelies** can be discovered between pages 6 and 114. They've been grouped into families, arranged in alphabetical order. First up are the fabulous **Brunch Nums**, followed by the **Candy cuties** .... all the way up to those **vital Veggies**.

Want s'more? You can learn about the **Noms** on pages 115 to 155. **Erase-Its, Gloss-Ups, Go-Gos, Light-Ups,** and **Stamp-Its** .... you'll find them all here! And if you're having trouble tracking down a particular **Num Nom,** turn to the Index on page 156 to find your faves.

POPPing Off

Have you met Pip, Pup, and Pop Corn? These excitable Eraser Noms are never in one place for too long! You can read all about them on page 116. But they've also gone to check out the Nums and are hiding on three different pages in this Collector's Guide. Can you track down all of them? Answers are on page 160.

FOOD for Thought

Flavorsome Fact
Fun nuggets of info about all the Nums and Noms.

Scent
From bacon to wildberry, discover each Num Nom's scent here.

Special Edition
This sign appears by all rare Num Noms.

Cute Quote
Want to hear the Num Noms' thoughts? Yes, peas!

Series
Dish-cover if your Num or Nom belongs to Series 1, 2, 3, or Lights 1.

Glittery Berry Go-Go

Special EDITION

- FLAVORSOME FACT: Prepare to meet the glitziest Go-Go on the block. Glittery Berry's sparkling sense of humor is a berry big hit among the glitter-raspberries.
- CUTE QUOTE: "All of my friends say I have a twinkle in my eye."
- SCENT: Raspberry
- SERIES: 2
- CHARACTER NUMBER: 2-106
- BFF: Strawberry Cream (Cupcake)

I have ◯

Character Number
Each Num Nom has a unique number. You can also find these on the handy checklist in each pack.

BFF
Everyone needs a best friend. So do the Num Noms . . . some even have two! You can see who matches up here.

I have (Check Box)
Keep track of your collection by checking the circle next to all the Num Noms you have. See which ones you still need if you want to complete a whole family.

Brunch NUMS

These sweet and savory treats will make your morning . . . but they're always cute whatever the time of day!

I have ◯

StrawBerry Froyo

- FLAVORSOME FACT: You can never be sure about Strawberry's mood. Usually she's super-sweet, but sometimes she can be tart!
- CUTE QUOTE: "I look cold on the outside, but I've got a warm heart"
- SCENT: Strawberry
- SERIES: 2
- CHARACTER NUMBER: 2-007
- BFF: Creamy Pop (Freezie Pop)

Cindy Cinnamon

- FLAVORSOME FACT: Cindy is one of the upper-crust Nums. Luckily, she's not short of money . . . she was born rolling in the dough!
- CUTE QUOTE: "No other Num smells like me. I STICK out from the rest!"
- SCENT: Cinnamon
- SERIES: 2
- CHARACTER NUMBER: 2-004
- BFF: Berry Cakes (Brunch)

I have ◯

Willy Waffles

- FLAVORSOME FACT: Willy is not very good at making decisions. The other Nums often fall asleep when he's talking to them. When they wake up, hours later, Willy is still waffling on!
- CUTE QUOTE: "Strawberries are the best fruit. Although, blueberries are great. No, it's strawberries. I think . . ."
- SCENT: Waffle
- SERIES: 2
- CHARACTER NUMBER: 2-003
- BFF: Jammin' Razzy Go-Go (Nom)

I have ◯

Becca Bacon

- FLAVORSOME FACT: Life is never dull for the other Num Noms if Becca's around. When she arrives, things start to sizzle!
- CUTE QUOTE: "If something goes wrong, you should never give up. My motto is always fry, fry, and fry again!"
- SCENT: Bacon
- SERIES: 2
- CHARACTER NUMBER: 2-006
- BFF: Melty Burger (Diner Food)

I have ◯

I have ◯

Nilla Froyo

- **FLAVORSOME FACT:** This green gal is definitely in the know-yo. She has the dish on all the great places to visit ... especially if you want the best spot for treats.
- **CUTE QUOTE:** "I'll take you to the coolest, freshest venues in town."
- **SCENT:** Vanilla
- **SERIES:** 2
- **CHARACTER NUMBER:** 2-008
- **BFF:** B-Day Gummy Stamp-It (Nom)

Berry cakes

- **FLAVORSOME FACT:** Beautiful Berry Cakes just loves to make sweet music. She does sing a little flat now and again. But she doesn't care, even if the odds are stacked against her.
- **CUTE QUOTE:** "Hey, who are you callin' flat? I'm berry popular, you know."
- **SCENT:** Blueberry
- **SERIES:** 2
- **CHARACTER NUMBER:** 2-002
- **BFF:** Cindy Cinnamon (Brunch)

I have ◯

Sunny Omelette

- FLAVORSOME FACT: This little Num sees the sunny side of life. She loves hanging with her BFF, Eggbert, and always cracks up listening to his egg-cellent puns.
- CUTE QUOTE: "Guess I must be pretty talented because I often hear the other Nums calling me egg-straordinary."
- SCENT: Egg
- SERIES: 2
- CHARACTER NUMBER: 2-005
- BFF: Eggbert Tamago (Sushi)

I have ◯

Berry Waffles

- FLAVORSOME FACT: It's time to say "Good Morning" to Berry Waffles. She makes everyone feel batter. You're going to love her sweet company at any time of day.
- CUTE QUOTE: "Aw, that's kind of you to say. I like you a-waffle lot, too."
- SCENT: Strawberry
- SERIES: 2
- CHARACTER NUMBER: 2-010
- BFF: Wild Berry Gummy Stamp-It (Nom)

Special **EDITION**

I have ◯

9

maple cakes

I have ◯

- **FLAVORSOME FACT:** This little Num knows that pancakes are the greatest. You can't get batter than that! Maple gets super-excited at mealtimes, but by Sunday brunch she has totally flipped out.
- **CUTE QUOTE:** "Aw, enough already. . . . I pan-cake any more excitement today!"
- **SCENT:** Pancake
- **SERIES:** 2
- **CHARACTER NUMBER:** 2-001
- **BFF:** Buttery Go-Go (Nom)

Flap Jackie

- **FLAVORSOME FACT:** Don't get in a flap about it, but this gleeful Num has stacks of ideas for fancy flavor combos. However, her suggestions can be rather surprising. . . .
- **CUTE QUOTE:** "Hmm, shall we combine . . . Wasabi Go-Go with Becca Bacon, Lulu Licorice, and me? Bet no one's tried that!"
- **SCENT:** Birthday cake
- **SERIES:** 2
- **CHARACTER NUMBER:** 2-123
- **BFF:** Ricky Roll (Brunch)

Special **EDITION**

I have ◯

Berry Froyo

- FLAVORSOME FACT: Berry is so popular, the other Nums write poetry about her. With her cute little curl and her big purple swirl, she'll put your head in a whirl, girl!
- CUTE QUOTE: "All of my friends are berry sweet. They never freeze me out!"
- SCENT: Blueberry
- SERIES: 2
- CHARACTER NUMBER: 2-009
- BFF: Berrylicious Gloss-Up (Nom)

I have ◯

Ricky Roll

- FLAVORSOME FACT: Do you like a jam session? You've found the right Num. Ricky loves getting down to old-school music. When those classic 1980s tunes come on, she really starts to roll. She'll never give you up. . . .
- CUTE QUOTE: "I'll never run around and dessert you."
- SCENT: Raspberry
- SERIES: 2
- CHARACTER NUMBER: 2-127
- BFF: Flap Jackie (Brunch)

Special **EDITION**

I have ◯

CANDY NUMS

Are you ready to meet the treats?
These colorful cuties prove
that candy really is dandy.

I have ◯

Sparkle Mellie

- **FLAVORSOME FACT:** Are you feeling a little melon-choly? Having a hard time? Then add some sparkle to your life with this cute candy.
- **CUTE QUOTE:** "There's no rind or reason to the things I do."
- **SCENT:** Watermelon
- **SERIES:** 3
- **CHARACTER NUMBER:** 3-047
- **BFF:** Cucumber Melon Gloss-Up (Nom)

Gabby Grape

- **FLAVORSOME FACT:** Sympathetic Gabby is a grape friend. She is a good listener, and her friends can talk to her whenever they want.
- **CUTE QUOTE:** "There's no need to whine about anything, sugarplum."
- **SCENT:** Grape
- **SERIES:** 3
- **CHARACTER NUMBER:** 3-057
- **BFF:** Rockie S. Berry (Candy)

I have ◯

Peyton Peppermint

- **FLAVORSOME FACT:** Lovely Peyton Peppermint is famous among the other Num Noms for always being sweet. She's a true friend . . . she never changes her stripes.
- **CUTE QUOTE:** "When my BFF has her birthday, I always send her sweet scent-a-mints."
- **SCENT:** Peppermint
- **SERIES:** 3
- **CHARACTER NUMBER:** 3-058
- **BFF:** Minty Mallow (Marshmallow)

I have

Mia Mango

- **FLAVORSOME FACT:** Mia Mango is a sucker for a tall tale. She loves stories with colorful characters who overcome hard knocks. And there must be a sweet ending.
- **CUTE QUOTE:** "When it comes to the crunch, I feel like I'm going to pieces."
- **SCENT:** Mango
- **SERIES:** 3
- **CHARACTER NUMBER:** 3-059
- **BFF:** Melon Gummy Stamp-It (Nom)

I have

I have ◯

? RainBow POP

- 🍬 FLAVORSOME FACT: Wow, this little lady has a whole rainbow of flavors to share with you. But what are they? She'll never tell because she takes pride in being a bit of a mystery.
- 🍬 CUTE QUOTE: "Want to find out more about me? Sorry, my lips are sealed."
- 🍬 SCENT: Mystery
- 🍬 SERIES: 3
- 🍬 CHARACTER NUMBER: 3-062
- 🍬 BFF: Brooklyn Blue (Candy)

Lily Lemony

- 🍬 FLAVORSOME FACT: Don't be fooled by her pretty exterior. Lily Lemony's head isn't just full of sweet nothings . . . she can wrap her mind around any problem.
- 🍬 CUTE QUOTE: "Lemme tell you, sweetie, I earned my stripes the hard way."
- 🍬 SCENT: Lemon
- 🍬 SERIES: 3
- 🍬 CHARACTER NUMBER: 3-056
- 🍬 BFF: Berry Gummy Stamp-It (Nom)

I have ◯

Candy Hearts

- 🍬 FLAVORSOME FACT: With her sweet nature and kind heart, you'll fall in love with Candy. She's one Num you'll want to cherry-ish.
- 🍬 CUTE QUOTE: "Aw, come here and give me a cuddle . . . it's Free Hugs Friday!"
- 🍬 SCENT: Cherry
- 🍬 SERIES: 3
- 🍬 CHARACTER NUMBER: 3-051
- 🍬 BFF: Nana Hearts (Candy)

I have ◯

Sugar Stripes

- 🍬 FLAVORSOME FACT: Straight-talking Sugar is berry direct with the other Num Noms and doesn't candy-coat anything she says.
- 🍬 CUTE QUOTE: "There's nothing sweeter than spending time with friends."
- 🍬 SCENT: Strawberry
- 🍬 SERIES: 3
- 🍬 CHARACTER NUMBER: 3-049
- 🍬 BFF: Strawberry Mallow (Marshmallow)

I have ◯

Brooklyn Blue

- 🍬 FLAVORSOME FACT: Once in a blue moon, a Candy comes along to sweeten your day. And here she is . . . Ms. Brooklyn Blue.
- 🍬 CUTE QUOTE: "Blue lobsters are my favorite animals. Or peacocks. Or maybe blue whales."
- 🍬 SCENT: Blue raspberry
- 🍬 SERIES: 3
- 🍬 CHARACTER NUMBER: 3-060
- 🍬 BFF: Rainbow Pop (Candy)

I have ◯

I have ◯

courtney candy

- FLAVORSOME FACT: Despite her sweet and fluffy reputation, Courtney Candy has firm views on everything. And she's not afraid to make her opinions crystal clear.
- CUTE QUOTE: "Hold on, I just need a moment to crystallize my thoughts."
- SCENT: Cotton Candy
- SERIES: 3
- CHARACTER NUMBER: 3-050
- BFF: Sugary Glaze (Donut)

Tina Tangerine

- FLAVORSOME FACT: Clever Tina Tangerine is a real high achiever. She gets good grades in all her classes, making everything look as easy as taking candy from a baby.
- CUTE QUOTE: "Listen up, guys! If you work hard, you're sure to get some sweet rewards. That's my motto."
- SCENT: Orange
- SERIES: 3
- CHARACTER NUMBER: 3-052
- BFF: Orange Piña Gloss-Up (Nom)

I have ◯

Swirls Lolly

- 🍬 **FLAVORSOME FACT:** With her swirly pink stripes and cute purple bow, Swirls looks and smells like a treat! And as a lollipop, this adorable Num makes great arm candy.
- 🍬 **CUTE QUOTE:** "Lollipops don't pop, but bubblegum bubbles do. It's so confusing!"
- 🍬 **SCENT:** Bubblegum
- 🍬 **SERIES:** 3
- 🍬 **CHARACTER NUMBER:** 3-061
- 🍬 **BFF:** Glitter Surprise Gloss-Up (Nom)

I have ◯

Crystal W. Berry

- 🍬 **FLAVORSOME FACT:** If you looked into a crystal ball, you'd see that there's more to this Num than meets the eye. It's clear that Crystal has a sweet side and a wild side.
- 🍬 **CUTE QUOTE:** "The W stands for either wild or wonderful. Maybe I can be both."
- 🍬 **SCENT:** Wildberry
- 🍬 **SERIES:** 3
- 🍬 **CHARACTER NUMBER:** 3-054
- 🍬 **BFF:** Marsha Violet (Marshmallow)

I have ◯

Suzy Stripes

- **FLAVORSOME FACT:** Fun-loving Suzy adores birthday celebrations. She gets so excited that when party time comes around she's like a kid in a candy store.
- **CUTE QUOTE:** "It's hard to keep me in line."
- **SCENT:** Birthday cake
- **SERIES:** 3
- **CHARACTER NUMBER:** 3-048
- **BFF:** Sprinkles Donut (Donut)

I have ◯

Rockie S. Berry

- **FLAVORSOME FACT:** Rockie S. Berry is a real hard candy. She won't stick to the music when rehearsing . . . she totally rocks out.
- **CUTE QUOTE:** "I like my music the same as I like my candy . . . hard rock"
- **SCENT:** Strawberry
- **SERIES:** 3
- **CHARACTER NUMBER:** 3-053
- **BFF:** Gabby Grape (Candy)

I have ◯

Nana Hearts

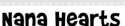

- **FLAVORSOME FACT:** Affectionate Nana Hearts loves to show her friends how much she cares about them.
- **CUTE QUOTE:** "You stole a piece of my heart, so I've got a bunch of hugs for you"
- **SCENT:** Banana
- **SERIES:** 3
- **CHARACTER NUMBER:** 3-055
- **BFF:** Candy Hearts (Candy)

I have ◯

CUPCAKE NUMS

Super-cute and oh so sweet, these scrumptious-smelling Num Noms are like a little piece of heaven just for you.

Special **EDITION**

I have ◯

Minty Swirl

- FLAVORSOME FACT: Minty's friends love her because she has their backs 100 per-scent. She's always full of encourage-mint.
- CUTE QUOTE: "I tell my pals they've gotta have a positive mint-ality."
- SCENT: Mint
- SERIES: 1
- CHARACTER NUMBER: 119
- BFF: Minty Chip (Ice Cream)

Patty Peach

- FLAVORSOME FACT: Patty Peach just loves to hang out with her best buddies. It always gives her a warm, fuzzy feeling.
- CUTE QUOTE: "When I'm not with my friends, life is just the pits."
- SCENT: Peach
- SERIES: 1
- CHARACTER NUMBER: 108
- BFF: Peachy Gloss-Up (Nom)

I have ◯

RaspBerry Cream

- **FLAVORSOME FACT:** Pink is Raspberry's favorite color . . . LOTS of pink. It makes her very happy, cuz she really is a berry girly girl.
- **CUTE QUOTE:** "Wait a minute. I like other colors, too. I also love magenta, salmon, fuchsia, coral, and rose . . ."
- **SCENT:** Raspberry
- **SERIES:** 1
- **CHARACTER NUMBER:** 114
- **BFF:** Peachy Cream (Ice Cream)

I have ⬭

Sugar Berry

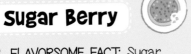

- **FLAVORSOME FACT:** Sugar loves to bake and share with her friends. She always serves up a sweet treat.
- **CUTE QUOTE:** "Never be afraid to try something new. Life is what you bake it. That's what I always say."
- **SCENT:** Sugar cookie
- **SERIES:** 2
- **CHARACTER NUMBER:** 2-070
- **BFFS:** Gingerbread Go-Go (Nom)

Special **EDITION**

I have ⬭

I have ◯

M. Mallow

FLAVORSOME FACT: M. Mallow enjoys getting toasty by a warm fire on a cold night. Her friends adore her tales .... except when she gets a bit too mallow-dramatic.

CUTE QUOTE: "What do you mean? They LOVE my stories. I'm on fire here!"

SCENT: Marshmallow

SERIES: 2

CHARACTER NUMBER: 2-065

BFF: Icy Piña Go-Go (Nom)

Cheery Cherie

FLAVORSOME FACT: This happy little Num brings a cupcake of good cheer wherever she goes. She thinks that everything is better with a cherry on top .... and maybe a few choco sprinkles, too!

CUTE QUOTE: "If you've had an argument, try not to stay angry. I believe you should kiss and bake up"

SCENT: Cherry

SERIES: 1

CHARACTER NUMBER: 112

BFF: Lulu Licorice (Ice Cream)

I have ◯

Cherry ChoCo

- **FLAVORSOME FACT:** Cherry is one of the sweetest Num Noms. In fact, she loves sweets so much that she thinks dessert should come before dinner!
- **CUTE QUOTE:** "Never save the best until last . . . have it first instead!"
- **SCENT:** Chocolate
- **SERIES:** 1
- **CHARACTER NUMBER:** 118
- **BFF:** Red Velvety (Cupcake)

I have ◯

Lemony Burst

- **FLAVORSOME FACT:** Whether it's making friends or exploring somewhere new, Lemony Burst is ready to join in. She has a real zest for life!
- **CUTE QUOTE:** "I never run out of juice. I'm always up for another adventure."
- **SCENT:** Lemon
- **SERIES:** 1
- **CHARACTER NUMBER:** 105
- **BFF:** Tropical Go-Go (Nom)

I have ◯

Nana Swirl

- **FLAVORSOME FACT:** Nana Swirl finds making up her mind tricky. She always makes split decisions! But she'll be best buds with Nana Pop forever.
- **CUTE QUOTE:** "Everyone loves bananas. They have lots of ap-peel!"
- **SCENT:** Banana
- **SERIES:** 2
- **CHARACTER NUMBER:** 2-063
- **BFF:** Nana Pop (Freezie Pop)

I have ◯

Candie Puffs

I have ◯

- **FLAVORSOME FACT:** Candie is a real thrill-seeker and loves the rides at the carnival. She enjoys living the high life on the roller coaster, but the Tilt-A-Whirl is her favorite. That's because she always enjoys being in a spin!
- **CUTE QUOTE:** "I love going on a round trip!"
- **SCENT:** Cotton candy
- **SERIES:** 1
- **CHARACTER NUMBER:** 120
- **BFF:** Bonnie Blueberry (Cupcake)

Betsy Bubblegum

- **FLAVORSOME FACT:** Some friends float away, but not Betsy Bubblegum. This cutie is always loyal to her pals. She sticks by them, especially her bestie, Mintee.
- **CUTE QUOTE:** "What chew up to? Let me put my gumboots on and I'll come and help"
- **SCENT:** Bubblegum
- **SERIES:** 1
- **CHARACTER NUMBER:** 111
- **BFF:** Mintee Gloss-up (Nom)

I have ◯

I have ◯

StrawBerry cream

- FLAVORSOME FACT: Meet Strawberry Cream. All the girlies stare at this special fella because they think he's creamy . . . that's why he's always blushing.
- CUTE QUOTE: "I'm not blushing. I just get a little shiny on a hot day."
- SCENT: Strawberry
- SERIES: 2
- CHARACTER NUMBER: 2-068
- BFF: Glittery Berry Go-Go (Nom)

Mrs. Icing ?

- FLAVORSOME FACT: Here comes the bride! Mrs. Icing is devoted to her husband, and they've always been sweethearts. When you love like they do, happiness is a piece of cake.
- CUTE QUOTE: "Love is like the icing on the cake of life, don'tcha think, sweetie?"
- SCENT: Mystery
- SERIES: 2
- CHARACTER NUMBER: 2-134
- BFF: Mr. Icing (Nom)

I have ◯

Pinkie Lemonade

- **FLAVORSOME FACT:** There are two sides to Pinkie Lemonade. She's usually sparkling and sweet, but watch out for her bad moods . . . she can be a bit sour.
- **CUTE QUOTE:** "I've got so many great ideas just bubbling away."
- **SCENT:** Pink lemonade
- **SERIES:** 1
- **CHARACTER NUMBER:** 106
- **BFF:** Wendy Wild Berry (Cupcake)

I have ◯

Wendy Wild Berry

- **FLAVORSOME FACT:** Judging by her name, you might expect that Wendy would be a real wild child. But to tell the truth, she's actually berry tame.
- **CUTE QUOTE:** "You know, I'm just sooo wild that I actually wore my bow on the OTHER side of my head last week. No, really. I did."
- **SCENT:** Blueberry
- **SERIES:** 1
- **CHARACTER NUMBER:** 116
- **BFF:** Pinkie Lemonade (Cupcake)

I have ◯

I have ◯

Choco Berry

- **FLAVORSOME FACT:** Here comes shy guy Choco Berry. He's a berry sensitive soul and loud noises make him go to pieces. When he wants some quiet time, he likes to hide in heart-shaped boxes.
- **CUTE QUOTE:** "You're special. You'll always have a piece of my chocolate heart"
- **SCENT:** Chocolate
- **SERIES:** 1
- **CHARACTER NUMBER:** 123
- **BFF:** Berry Gloss-Up (Nom)

Nilla Swirl

- **FLAVORSOME FACT:** Nilla Swirl worries about everything from her scent to which side her bow looks best. This poor Num often makes half-baked plans and then crumbles under the pressure.
- **CUTE QUOTE:** "Aaargh! I can't stand all this stress. It's bakin' me crazy!"
- **SCENT:** Vanilla
- **SERIES:** 1
- **CHARACTER NUMBER:** 102
- **BFF:** Mary Mulberry (Cupcake)

I have ◯

Caramelly Shine

- **FLAVORSOME FACT:** This little honey bunny is Miss Caramelly Shine. She looks and smells so good that there's just no topping her sweetness.
- **CUTE QUOTE:** "It's time to rise and shine . . . and I should know all about that!"
- **SCENT:** Caramel
- **SERIES:** 2
- **CHARACTER NUMBER:** 2-071
- **BFF:** Choco Swirl (Cupcake)

Special **EDITION**

I have ◯

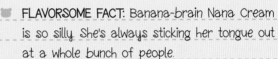

Nana Cream

- **FLAVORSOME FACT:** Banana-brain Nana Cream is so silly. She's always sticking her tongue out at a whole bunch of people.
- **CUTE QUOTE:** "Well, there's muffin else to do around here."
- **SCENT:** Banana
- **SERIES:** 1
- **CHARACTER NUMBER:** 104
- **BFF:** Billy Banana (Ice Cream)

I have ◯

Sweetie StrawBerry

- **FLAVORSOME FACT:** This Num is such a little sweetie. She is a great friend to everyone and can see the good in even the baddest seeds.
- **CUTE QUOTE:** "Sweet strawberries from little seeds grow. That's my slogan."
- **SCENT:** Strawberry
- **SERIES:** 1
- **CHARACTER NUMBER:** 110
- **BFF:** Lemony Go-Go (Nom)

I have ◯

Berry Cheesecake

- FLAVORSOME FACT: This Num is berry good in the kitchen. Although cheese obsessed with baking, she doesn't like doing it by herself. It's all about teamwork, which is why she never desserts her friends.
- CUTE QUOTE: "Hey, guys, ricotta get together again real soon."
- SCENT: Wildberry
- SERIES: 2
- CHARACTER NUMBER: 2-064
- BFF: Mozza Rella (Pizza)

I have

Orange Swirl

- FLAVORSOME FACT: This zesty little Num Nom is so full of life. Wherever she goes, she always has a bounce in her step. Even when she's squeezed for time, she gets everything done.
- CUTE QUOTE: "It's a busy day. I'd better get ready to spruce up my juice."
- SCENT: Orange
- SERIES: 1
- CHARACTER NUMBER: 107
- BFF: Bailey Bubblegum (Ice Cream)

I have

Betty B-Day

- **FLAVORSOME FACT:** Party animal Betty doesn't need an excuse for a get-together with friends. For her, there's something special happening every day.
- **CUTE QUOTE:** "What's that? It's exactly one year since we met? That's worth celebrating! Right, we'll need balloons, party hats, decorations. . . "
- **SCENT:** Birthday cake
- **SERIES:** 1
- **CHARACTER NUMBER:** 122
- **BFF:** Bubbly Go-Go (Nom)

I have ◯

Mary Mulberry

- **FLAVORSOME FACT:** The other Num Noms need to mauve over and make room for Mary. If you can't find her, she's sure to be hanging around the mulberry bush.
- **CUTE QUOTE:** "My favorite way to relax is to berry myself in a nature book."
- **SCENT:** Wildberry
- **SERIES:** 1
- **CHARACTER NUMBER:** 115
- **BFF:** Nilla Swirl (Cupcake)

I have ◯

Choco Swirl

- **FLAVORSOME FACT:** Laid-back Choco Swirl always heads straight to the beach for her summer vacation. She just loves to melt in the hot sun.
- **CUTE QUOTE:** "Better choco-late than never."
- **SCENT:** Chocolate
- **SERIES:** 2
- **CHARACTER NUMBER:** 2-069
- **BFF:** Caramelly Shine (Cupcake)

Special **EDITION**

I have ◯

Mint Berry

- **FLAVORSOME FACT:** When the other Cupcake Nums have worries, they can talk to Mint Berry. She always listens without judge-mint.
- **CUTE QUOTE:** "I mint to say that was a berry nice thing to do."
- **SCENT:** Mint
- **SERIES:** 2
- **CHARACTER NUMBER:** 2-066
- **BFF:** Mint Gummy Stamp-It (Nom)

 I have ◯

Mimi Mango

- **FLAVORSOME FACT:** Mimi Mango is always jetting off to exotic locations. She loves catching the last rays of the day.
- **CUTE QUOTE:** "Bring on the heat! I always savor a tropical flavor."
- **SCENT:** Mango
- **SERIES:** 1
- **CHARACTER NUMBER:** 109
- **BFF:** Neo Trio (Ice Cream)

I have ◯

Berry Berry Swirl

- **FLAVORSOME FACT:** With her love of pink candy necklaces and lollipop rings, this likable Num is a real candy girl. There's muffin more she likes to do than wear all her jewelry at once.
- **CUTE QUOTE:** "You're not seeing double. I'm so sweet they named me twice."
- **SCENT:** Strawberry
- **SERIES:** 1
- **CHARACTER NUMBER:** 113
- **BFF:** Nana Gloss-Up (Nom)

I have ⬡

Red Velvety

- **FLAVORSOME FACT:** Red Velvety really is something special. This crimson cutie loves Valentine's Day because she's a softie at heart.
- **CUTE QUOTE:** "Aw, stop it . . . have I gone red? I can feel myself blushing again. I think I'd better beet it until I've cooled down."
- **SCENT:** Red velvet
- **SERIES:** 1
- **CHARACTER NUMBER:** 121
- **BFF:** Cherry Choco (Cupcake)

Special **EDITION**

I have ⬡

I have ◯

Nilla Cream

- **FLAVORSOME FACT:** If you want the recipe for happiness, this cutie might be able to help you out. Sweet-smelling Nilla Cream is always smiling. That's because her Num Nom friends call her "the cream of the crop."
- **CUTE QUOTE:** "Yup, and I always rise to the top!"
- **SCENT:** Vanilla
- **SERIES:** 1
- **CHARACTER NUMBER:** 101
- **BFF:** Cherry Go-Go (Nom)

Cherry Cheesecake

- **FLAVORSOME FACT:** Daring Cherry Cheesecake often gets herself into sticky situations. But whichever way you slice it, she always comes out smelling good.
- **CUTE QUOTE:** "My friends call me Miss Cheese-ius. Guess that's because I'm always up to something!"
- **SCENT:** Cherry
- **SERIES:** 2
- **CHARACTER NUMBER:** 2-067
- **BFF:** Cherry Jelly Go-Go (Nom)

Special **EDITION**

I have ◯

Mara Schino

- FLAVORSOME FACT: Despite her appearance, Mara Schino rarely sees red. For this little Num, life is like a bowl of cherries.
- CUTE QUOTE: "You guys are so sweet . . . you really take the cake!"
- SCENT: Cherry
- SERIES: 2
- CHARACTER NUMBER: 2-120
- BFF: Nilla Crème Gloss-Up (Nom)

Special **EDITION**

I have ◯

ChoCo Nana

- FLAVORSOME FACT: Watch out, girls, Choco Nana is here. With his wink and smile, he makes all the ladies go mushy.
- CUTE QUOTE: "I might have a hard shell, but it doesn't take much to make me melt"
- SCENT: Banana
- SERIES: 1
- CHARACTER NUMBER: 103
- BFF: Mintee Go-Go (Nom)

I have ◯

Bonnie BlueBerry

- FLAVORSOME FACT: Now, don't you worry about Bonnie Blueberry. She may be blue, but she really is a berry happy bunny.
- CUTE QUOTE: "Yippee! Treats make me jump for joy!"
- SCENT: Blueberry
- SERIES: 1
- CHARACTER NUMBER: 117
- BFF: Candie Puffs (Cupcake)

I have ◯

Diner Food Nums

Slide into a booth and spend some fun time with the Diner Food Nums. They've got so much to tell you, you'll quickly ketchup on all the gossip!

I have ◯

Lemony Cola

- **FLAVORSOME FACT:** Lemony Cola's bubbly personality is like a cool drink on a hot day.
- **CUTE QUOTE:** "I soda think you're amazing, too."
- **SCENT:** Lemon soda
- **SERIES:** 2
- **CHARACTER NUMBER:** 2-033
- **BFFS:** Frenchie Curls (Diner Food) and Hammy Burger (Diner Food)

Haley Hot Dog

- **FLAVORSOME FACT:** Hot diggity dog, have you met Haley? She's no silly sausage. In fact, she's more than a little frank. Just don't get in a bun-fight with her.
- **CUTE QUOTE:** "Yo, dawg, that cuts no mustard with me."
- **SCENT:** Hot dog
- **SERIES:** 2
- **CHARACTER NUMBER:** 2-029
- **BFF:** Margo Rita (Pizza)

I have ◯

I have ◯

Hammy Burger

- **FLAVORSOME FACT:** Hammy is always on a roll. He's not sure if he prefers hanging out with Frenchie Curls or Lemony Cola, so he's super-sized his BFF choice and has two!
- **CUTE QUOTE:** "I'm off to dance at the meat ball!"
- **SCENT:** Burger
- **SERIES:** 2
- **CHARACTER NUMBER:** 2-027
- **BFFS:** Frenchie Curls (Diner Food) and Lemony Cola (Diner Food)

B.L.T.

- **FLAVORSOME FACT:** Yawn! Sleepyhead B.L.T. is always telling the other Num Noms to get more rest. She's not being bossy; she's just trying to bacon-structive.
- **CUTE QUOTE:** "I'm bacon you to lettuce take a nap because I'm tired from my head to-ma-toes."
- **SCENT:** Bacon
- **SERIES:** 2
- **CHARACTER NUMBER:** 2-036
- **BFF:** Suki Sake (Sushi)

Special **EDITION**

I have ◯

I have ◯

Frenchie Fries

- **FLAVORSOME FACT:** Frenchie is the small fry with big dreams. She's no couch potato; she longs to travel. France would be perfect since she wants to get back to her roots.
- **CUTE QUOTE:** "It's true that I have French connections, but I haven't got a chip on my shoulder about it"
- **SCENT:** Fries
- **SERIES:** 2
- **CHARACTER NUMBER:** 2-030
- **BFF:** Ketchup Go-Go (Nom)

C.H.Z.

- **FLAVORSOME FACT:** If you ever feel worried, don't panic . . . C.H.Z. will be there to comfort you. With her bright and brie-zy personality and Gouda heart, she makes all her friends melt.
- **CUTE QUOTE:** "It ain't easy being cheesy, but I guess I cheddar get used to it"
- **SCENT:** Cheese
- **SERIES:** 2
- **CHARACTER NUMBER:** 2-035
- **BFF:** Grape Jelly Go-Go (Nom)

I have ◯

cassie cola

- FLAVORSOME FACT: Bubbly Cassie Cola is soda-lightful. Her sparkling wit always goes down well with the other Diner Food Nums. They look up to her because she's the liter of the pack.
- CUTE QUOTE: "I don't need much. When I go on vacation, I always pack lite."
- SCENT: Cola soda
- SERIES: 2
- CHARACTER NUMBER: 2-032
- BFF: Icy Berry Go-Go (Nom)

I have ◯

P.B.N.J.

- FLAVORSOME FACT: This Num is a big hit in the Diner, cuz when her jam plays on the radio, she cuts some really smooth moves.
- CUTE QUOTE: "Spread out, guys, and watch me in action. It does nut get any butter than this."
- SCENT: Blueberry
- SERIES: 2
- CHARACTER NUMBER: 2-034
- BFF: Jammin' Berry Go-Go (Nom)

I have ◯

I have ◯

Melty Burger

- **FLAVORSOME FACT:** Make no minced-steak . . . although Melty Burger is a little cheesy, it's not rare to hear that he's done well. He likes nothing more than having a discussion with his friends and giving them a good grilling.
- **CUTE QUOTE:** "I always think outside the bun."
- **SCENT:** Cheese
- **SERIES:** 2
- **CHARACTER NUMBER:** 2-028
- **BFF:** Becca Bacon (Brunch)

Frenchie Curls

- **FLAVORSOME FACT:** Even though Frenchie Curls is small potatoes compared to some of the other Diner Food Nums, she's always sweet about it.
- **CUTE QUOTE:** "What's my favorite song? 'Curls Just Wanna Have Fun,' of course!"
- **SCENT:** Sweet potato fries
- **SERIES:** 2
- **CHARACTER NUMBER:** 2-031
- **BFFS:** Hammy Burger (Diner Food) and Lemony Cola (Diner Food)

I have ◯

Donut Nums

Serve up a hole lotta fun with the dreamy Donuts.
Who said these cuties aren't healthy?
They are hole foods, after all!

Choco Sprinkles

- **FLAVORSOME FACT:** When it comes to swimming, Choco is an expert in laps. He loves nothing more than taking a dip in a pool of milk.
- **CUTE QUOTE:** "Please sprinkle me with happiness"
- **SCENT:** Chocolate
- **SERIES:** 3
- **CHARACTER NUMBER:** 3-012
- **BFF:** Valerie Vanilla (Donut)

Orange Glaze

- **FLAVORSOME FACT:** Orange Glaze will tell you a tall tale or two. But you may find yourself glazing over, as her stories are often full of holes.
- **CUTE QUOTE:** "What do you mean you donut believe me?"
- **SCENT:** Orange
- **SERIES:** 3
- **CHARACTER NUMBER:** 3-007
- **BFF:** Lemony Glaze (Donut)

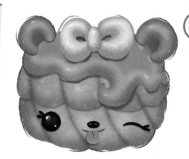

I have ◯

I have ◯

I have ◯

Sugary Glaze

- **FLAVORSOME FACT:** This sweet little thing just loves going to the carnival. And you can bet dollars to donuts that Sugary will be the first in line for all the rides.
- **CUTE QUOTE:** "I'm always first because no one can keep up with me. I run rings around all the other Donuts."
- **SCENT:** Cotton candy
- **SERIES:** 3
- **CHARACTER NUMBER:** 3-014
- **BFF:** Courtney Candy (Candy)

Razzi Berry

- **FLAVORSOME FACT:** Sparky Razzi Berry is jam-packed with attitude. She's bound to pick holes in any argument and make a list of all the doughs and donuts.
- **CUTE QUOTE:** "Whoa, are you sayin' that I got attitude, dude? Donut even get me started on that . . . "
- **SCENT:** Raspberry
- **SERIES:** 3
- **CHARACTER NUMBER:** 3-010
- **BFF:** Berry Stamp-It (Nom)

I have ◯

Sophia Strawberry

- FLAVORSOME FACT: Delightful Sophia is full of sweetness and light. She always makes time for friends. . . . This is one Num with a hole lotta love to give.
- CUTE QUOTE: "Donut worry, be happy . . . that's what I always say."
- SCENT: Strawberry
- SERIES: 3
- CHARACTER NUMBER: 3-003
- BFF: Van-Berry Gloss-Up (Nom)

I have ◯

Powdered Sugars

- FLAVORSOME FACT: If there's a party going on, this lively Num will be there. If she isn't shaking it up on the dance floor, she'll be powdering her nose in the bathroom.
- CUTE QUOTE: "Dust off your party clothes. Let's get ready for the hole shebang!"
- SCENT: Sugar cookie
- SERIES: 3
- CHARACTER NUMBER: 3-009
- BFF: Softy Mallow (Marshmallow)

I have ◯

Mac Minty

- **FLAVORSOME FACT:** Fancy a serious chat? Don't leaf out Mac Minty. This clear-headed Donut always has a fresh point of view.
- **CUTE QUOTE:** "You may think that I'm green about life, but I actually have a hole lot of common scents."
- **SCENT:** Mint
- **SERIES:** 3
- **CHARACTER NUMBER:** 3-004
- **BFF:** Trio Glow Cone (Snow Cone)

I have ◯

Lemony Glaze

- **FLAVORSOME FACT:** With sweet little Lemony, what you see on the surface is what you get. She's not self-centered at all. She puts so much energy into helping others . . . she has a real zest for it!
- **CUTE QUOTE:** "You look like you need some assistance. How about some lemon aid?"
- **SCENT:** Lemon
- **SERIES:** 3
- **CHARACTER NUMBER:** 3-011
- **BFF:** Orange Glaze (Donut)

I have ◯

I have ◯

Sprinkles Donut

- FLAVORSOME FACT: If you are planning a celebration, please donut forget to invite Sprinkles Donut. This lovable Num is so much fun, she should be at the topping of everyone's party list.
- CUTE QUOTE: "I just donut understand people who donut like to party."
- SCENT: Birthday cake
- SERIES: 3
- CHARACTER NUMBER: 3-013
- BFF: Suzy Stripes (Candy)

Cory Custard

- FLAVORSOME FACT: The other Num Noms say Cory is like "the happiness police." If you're wearing a frown, then she's sure to take you into custard-y.
- CUTE QUOTE: "Please donut give up if you are having a bad day . . . . you've got to have a positive attitude."
- SCENT: Custard
- SERIES: 3
- CHARACTER NUMBER: 3-001
- BFF: Toasty Mallow (Marshmallow)

I have ◯

I have ◯

WANDA WILDBERRY

- **FLAVORSOME FACT:** Most of Wanda Wildberry's friends think she is away with the berries. Sometimes she just stares ahead with a glazed expression on her face.
- **CUTE QUOTE:** "I know some of the other Nums are confused by me. I guess I'm just a tough donut to crack."
- **SCENT:** Wildberry
- **SERIES:** 3
- **CHARACTER NUMBER:** 3-005
- **BFF:** Cherry Ann (Donut)

Cherry Ann

- **FLAVORSOME FACT:** Most days, charming Cherry Ann just adores being one of the 14 Donut Nums. But occasionally, she does get tired of the hole thing.
- **CUTE QUOTE:** "Oh well, no sense moping around . . . I guess I'd batter make the most of it!"
- **SCENT:** Cherry
- **SERIES:** 3
- **CHARACTER NUMBER:** 3-002
- **BFF:** Wanda Wildberry (Donut)

I have ◯

I have ⃝

Valerie Vanilla

- 🐻 FLAVORSOME FACT: There are dozens of reasons why Valerie Vanilla loves cuddling up with her friends at home. It's difficult to extract her once she's there.
- 🐻 CUTE QUOTE: "I've bean waiting for you. You'll never get a frosty welcome from me. A frosting one, maybe!"
- 🐻 SCENT: Vanilla
- 🐻 SERIES: 3
- 🐻 CHARACTER NUMBER: 3-008
- 🐻 BFF: Choco Sprinkles (Donut)

Maple Sugars

- 🐻 FLAVORSOME FACT: Intrepid Maple loves taking a break from the city and heading for the great outdoors. For her, there's nothing batter than tapping into the sweet surprises of nature.
- 🐻 CUTE QUOTE: "Donut stay cooped up inside. There is a hole wide world out there."
- 🐻 SCENT: Maple
- 🐻 SERIES: 3
- 🐻 CHARACTER NUMBER: 3-006
- 🐻 BFF: Donut Stamp-It (Nom)

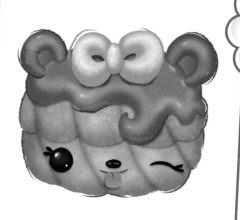

I have ⃝

Fair Food Nums

Roll up, roll up! Feast your eyes on these tempting treats . . . they'll have you running helter-skelter toward the fairground.

Annie Apple

- 🍬 FLAVORSOME FACT: You'll find sweet little Annie apple-y going about life. However, she does occasionally get herself into sticky situations.
- 🍬 CUTE QUOTE: "Uh-oh . . . this doesn't look good. I think it's crunch time."
- 🍬 SCENT: Caramel apple
- 🍬 SERIES: 2
- 🍬 CHARACTER NUMBER: 2-038
- 🍬 BFF: Caramel Stamp-It (Nom)

I have ◯

Sugar Puffs

- 🍬 FLAVORSOME FACT: With her cute, pink bow, Sugar Puffs is really very sweet. She does lack a little substance, though, because her head is full of fluff.
- 🍬 CUTE QUOTE: "Yeah, but fluffiness is cute, right?"
- 🍬 SCENT: Cotton candy
- 🍬 SERIES: 2
- 🍬 CHARACTER NUMBER: 2-040
- 🍬 BFF: Cotton Candy Gloss-Up (Nom)

I have ◯

Papa Corn

- **FLAVORSOME FACT:** Come and settle yourself down for one of Papa's a-maize-ing stories. However, it's best to take them with a pinch of salt because there's only a kernel of truth in the tales he tells.
- **CUTE QUOTE:** "Are you all corn-centrating? Terrific! I guarantee that this story will pop your mind. . . ."
- **SCENT:** Buttered popcorn
- **SERIES:** 2
- **CHARACTER NUMBER:** 2-042
- **BFF:** Momma Corn (Fair Food)

I have ◯

Pinky Puffs

- **FLAVORSOME FACT:** Adorable Pinky Puffs loves to go for a whirl on any fairground ride that spins her around and around. You'll always find her having a wheely good time.
- **CUTE QUOTE:** "Watch out . . . I can feel myself spiraling outta control!"
- **SCENT:** Cotton candy
- **SERIES:** 2
- **CHARACTER NUMBER:** 2-039
- **BFF:** Confetti Jelly (Jelly Bean)

I have ◯

I have ◯

Momma Corn

- **FLAVORSOME FACT:** Merry Momma Corn is famous among the other Num Noms for popping some terribly corny jokes. Momma doesn't realize that even her favorite jokes shuck.
- **CUTE QUOTE:** "Here's a good one! What did the baby corn say to the mommy corn? Where's my pop corn? Ha ha!"
- **SCENT:** Buttered popcorn
- **SERIES:** 2
- **CHARACTER NUMBER:** 2-043
- **BFF:** Papa Corn (Fair Food)

Twinzy Puffs

- **FLAVORSOME FACT:** If you're of two minds about which of the Fair Food Nums to choose, try to track down Twinzy Puffs. She's twice as nice!
- **CUTE QUOTE:** "There really are two sides to my personality . . . sweet and sweeter."
- **SCENT:** Cotton candy
- **SERIES:** 2
- **CHARACTER NUMBER:** 2-124
- **BFF:** Cotton Crème Gloss-Up (Nom)

I have ◯

I have ◯

cara Mellie

- 🐻 FLAVORSOME FACT: Whose side is mixed-up Cara Mellie on? She might keep the doctor away with her crisp, green apple half, but her sticky caramel side is bound to keep dentists happy!
- 🐻 CUTE QUOTE: "Hey, c'mon I'm no bad apple. How about a round of apple-ause?"
- 🐻 SCENT: Caramel apple
- 🐻 SERIES: 2
- 🐻 CHARACTER NUMBER: 2-037
- 🐻 BFF: Sammy S'mores (Pizza)

Nana Puffs

- 🐻 FLAVORSOME FACT: You're bound to have a whole bunch of fun if you hang out with Nana Puffs. When it comes to the Fair Foods, she really is top banana.
- 🐻 CUTE QUOTE: "Aw, is that a fluffy kitten picture I see? Cute things get me all mushy."
- 🐻 SCENT: Banana
- 🐻 SERIES: 2
- 🐻 CHARACTER NUMBER: 2-044
- 🐻 BFF: Cotton Candy Eraser (Nom)

Special EDITION

I have ◯

Berry Puffs

- 🐻 **FLAVORSOME FACT:** Poor little Berry is a bit puffy-eyed today. She knows when her friends get hungry she gets all pulled apart trying to help.
- 🐻 **CUTE QUOTE:** "When it comes to relaxing, I just wanna waft around the fairground, lookin' sweet."
- 🐻 **SCENT:** Blueberry
- 🐻 **SERIES:** 2
- 🐻 **CHARACTER NUMBER:** 2-041
- 🐻 **BFF:** Candy Gummy Stamp-It (Nom)

I have ◯

Auntie Corn

- 🐻 **FLAVORSOME FACT:** Good old Auntie Corn might seem like a laid-back Num, but she's just warming up. She's usually quiet for what seems like years, but suddenly she'll pop into action.
- 🐻 **CUTE QUOTE:** "Hi, sweetie. Why don't you pop over here and give Auntie a kiss?"
- 🐻 **SCENT:** Marshmallow
- 🐻 **SERIES:** 2
- 🐻 **CHARACTER NUMBER:** 2-122
- 🐻 **BFF:** Bubbly Pop (Freezie Pop)

Special **EDITION**

I have ◯

Fiesta Food Nums

Grab your maracas, it's fiesta time.
These sweet and savory snacks are all
the reason you need to celebrate. Olé!

I have ⬭

Berry Churro

- **FLAVORSOME FACT:** Say "Hola" to this special señorita. It's not easy to tell what she's thinking, but when she likes you, she says, "Churr-OK by me."
- **CUTE QUOTE:** "Who wants to go shopping? I've got the dough!"
- **SCENT:** Strawberry
- **SERIES:** 3
- **CHARACTER NUMBER:** 3-067
- **BFF:** Cheesy Burrito (Fiesta Food)

Cheesy Burrito

- **FLAVORSOME FACT:** Introducing Cheesy Burrito. This loca lady is crazy about street food. In fact, she's a little bit of a basket queso.
- **CUTE QUOTE:** "You can trust me . . . I'm not going to spill the beans"
- **SCENT:** Cheese bean burrito
- **SERIES:** 3
- **CHARACTER NUMBER:** 3-065
- **BFF:** Berry Churro (Fiesta Food)

I have ⬭

Tasty Taco

- **FLAVORSOME FACT:** The other Num Noms think that Tasty Taco is a little too full of himself. That's because he always loves to taco 'bout how awesome he is.
- **CUTE QUOTE:** "It's nacho problem."
- **SCENT:** Taco
- **SERIES:** 3
- **CHARACTER NUMBER:** 3-066
- **BFF:** Cinna Churro (Fiesta Food)

Special **EDITION**

I have ◯

Cinna Churro

- **FLAVORSOME FACT:** Cinna Churro loves hanging around amusement parks, but this sweet Num often ends up being the main attraction.
- **CUTE QUOTE:** "Life is always sweet when you roll in sugar and cinnamon."
- **SCENT:** Churro
- **SERIES:** 3
- **CHARACTER NUMBER:** 3-064
- **BFF:** Tasty Taco (Fiesta Food)

I have ◯

Flower Tortilla

- **FLAVORSOME FACT:** This little tortilla has got real flour power. And when it comes to yummy fillings, she's got it all wrapped up.
- **CUTE QUOTE:** "No way . . . you have guac to be kidding me."
- **SCENT:** Burrito
- **SERIES:** 3
- **CHARACTER NUMBER:** 3-063
- **BFF:** Carrie Corn (Veggie)

I have ◯

Freezie Pop Nums

Brrr! Time to cool off with some n-ice Nums. The Freezie Pops' fresh flavors are sure to chill you out.

I have ◯

 ## Grape Soda Pop

- **FLAVORSOME FACT:** Grape Soda Pop and her BFF are so similar. The same phrases pop out of their mouths because grape minds think alike!
- **CUTE QUOTE:** "I'm so grapeful to have such a fizzin' time with my BFF."
- **SCENT:** Grape
- **SERIES:** 2
- **CHARACTER NUMBER:** 2-054
- **BFF:** Grape Jelly (Jelly Bean)

Apple Pop

- **FLAVORSOME FACT:** Apple Pop is the perfect companion for a lovely summer's day . . . because when it's hot, she blows cold.
- **CUTE QUOTE:** "You'd be hard-pressed to meet a nicer Freezie than me."
- **SCENT:** Green apple
- **SERIES:** Lights 1
- **CHARACTER NUMBER:** L-028
- **BFF:** Pineapple Pop (Freezie Pop)

I have ◯

Mellie PoP

- **FLAVORSOME FACT:** Being the only red Freezie Pop, Mellie likes standing out from the crowd. She's happy being a unique Num Nom . . . in fact, she's one in a melon.
- **CUTE QUOTE:** "It doesn't bother me if it starts snowing. In fact, I like melon around in cold places."
- **SCENT:** Watermelon
- **SERIES:** 2
- **CHARACTER NUMBER:** 2-045
- **BFF:** Cucumber Gloss-Up (Nom)

I have ◯

Cherry Freezie

- **FLAVORSOME FACT:** When it comes to coping with new situations, Cherry Freezie usually has cold feet. But if it's something important, she'll force herself to shut her eyes tight and make a decision.
- **CUTE QUOTE:** "Leave it to me. I always try to look at the cold, hard facts."
- **SCENT:** Cherry
- **SERIES:** Lights 1
- **CHARACTER NUMBER:** L-025
- **BFF:** Cherry Light-Up (Nom)

I have ◯

I have ◯

Blue Razz Pop

- 🍬 FLAVORSOME FACT: Some say that Blue Razz is an ice maiden. You may mistake her for a cold piece of work at first, but when she defrosts a little, you'll find her freezie to get along with.
- 🍬 CUTE QUOTE: "I'm really not trying to freeze you out here, I prom-ice"
- 🍬 SCENT: Blue raspberry
- 🍬 SERIES: Lights 1
- 🍬 CHARACTER NUMBER: L-030
- 🍬 BFF: Sparkle Blueberry (Gummy)

Nana Pop

- 🍬 FLAVORSOME FACT: After a hard day skating on thin ice, Nana Pop needs to chill out. So she heads off to find a cool spot to relax in . . . it's very a-peel-ing!
- 🍬 CUTE QUOTE: "I take cold comfort in the freezer."
- 🍬 SCENT: Banana
- 🍬 SERIES: 2
- 🍬 CHARACTER NUMBER: 2-052
- 🍬 BFF: Nana Swirl (Cupcake)

I have ◯

Tropi-Cali POP

- FLAVORSOME FACT: This little freeze spirit is Tropi-Cali Pop. She might be striped because it's better than being spotted! Some say she has a cold heart, but she looks and feels like a tropical sunset.
- CUTE QUOTE: "It takes a while to know me. I have layers to my personality."
- SCENT: Mango
- SERIES: 2
- CHARACTER NUMBER: 2-049
- BFF: Chili Go-Go (Nom)

I have ◯

Lemony POP

- FLAVORSOME FACT: Little Lemony Pop is certainly one affectionate Num. Gaining new friends isn't a problem for her . . . she makes it look easy-peasy, lemon freezie. Her secret? She knows sour power is capable of anything!
- CUTE QUOTE: "Pucker up and lemme give you a kiss"
- SCENT: Lemon
- SERIES: 2
- CHARACTER NUMBER: 2-051
- BFF: OJ Pop (Freezie Pop)

I have ◯

StrawBerry POP

- **FLAVORSOME FACT:** When faced with a problem, Strawberry Pop always keeps a cool head. When she does make a decision, she sticks with it
- **CUTE QUOTE:** "I never freeze under pressure. I'm frozen already!"
- **SCENT:** Strawberry
- **SERIES:** 2
- **CHARACTER NUMBER:** 2-046
- **BFF:** Kiwi Jelly (Jelly Bean)

I have ◯

Orange Freezie

- **FLAVORSOME FACT:** Orange Freezie can light up any room. Whenever she senses an opportunity, she glows for it!
- **CUTE QUOTE:** "I believe that sherbet is a dish best served cold."
- **SCENT:** Orange
- **SERIES:** Lights 1
- **CHARACTER NUMBER:** L-026
- **BFF:** Orange Light-Up (Nom)

I have ◯

BuBBly POP

- **FLAVORSOME FACT:** Bubbly Pop is the most excitable Num around. Luckily, when her emotions bubble up, she cools down pretty quickly
- **CUTE QUOTE:** "I'm freeze 'n' easy and fun to chill out with."
- **SCENT:** Bubblegum
- **SERIES:** 2
- **CHARACTER NUMBER:** 2-121
- **BFF:** Auntie Corn (Fair Food)

Special **EDITION**

I have ◯

Kiwi Freezie

- **FLAVORSOME FACT:** The kiwi to this wonderful Num's heart is a nice meal. But she's more than happy with anything out of the freezer. She might not remember it the next day since she's known for being a little fuzzy.
- **CUTE QUOTE:** "That's just the tip of the ice-burgers."
- **SCENT:** Kiwi
- **SERIES:** 2
- **CHARACTER NUMBER:** 2-053
- **BFF:** Mango Jelly Go-Go (Nom)

I have ◯

Nea Pop

- **FLAVORSOME FACT:** Decisions, decisions! Nea Pop really struggles when she has to make a choice. So she tries a little of everything, just to be sure.
- **CUTE QUOTE:** "Don't get angry with me . . . it's a freeze country."
- **SCENT:** Chocolate
- **SERIES:** 2
- **CHARACTER NUMBER:** 2-126
- **BFF:** Nana Crème Gloss-Up (Nom)

Special **EDITION**

I have ◯

Creamy Pop

- **FLAVORSOME FACT:** Cool Creamy Pop loves to whip up excitement in everyone around her. And if she thinks they are giving her cold looks instead, she doesn't stick around.
- **CUTE QUOTE:** "Unfriendly people freeze my heart"
- **SCENT:** Strawberry
- **SERIES:** 2
- **CHARACTER NUMBER:** 2-047
- **BFF:** Strawberry Froyo (Brunch)

I have ◯

Wild Berry Freezie

- **FLAVORSOME FACT:** During the day, Wild Berry Freezie is a real cool cat. She usually spends her freeze time just chilling out, but at night she goes out to party the night away and show her berry wild side to the other Nums.
- **CUTE QUOTE:** "I go ice dancing all night long"
- **SCENT:** Blueberry
- **SERIES:** 2
- **CHARACTER NUMBER:** 2-048
- **BFF:** Oni Giri (Sushi)

I have ◯

Pineapple POP

- FLAVORSOME FACT: Pineapple Pop is a great friend and has a firm sense of right and wrong. She would never leave a pal out in the cold.
- CUTE QUOTE: "If someone is frosty with me, I'm totally crushed."
- SCENT: Pineapple
- SERIES: Lights 1
- CHARACTER NUMBER: L-027
- BFF: Apple Pop (Freezie Pop)

I have ◯

Grape Freezie

- FLAVORSOME FACT: This Num never feels the heat . . . she is one cool customer. If you need to chill, she'd be a grape friend to call on.
- CUTE QUOTE: "You know what they say . . . cold hands, warm heart."
- SCENT: Grape
- SERIES: Lights 1
- CHARACTER NUMBER: L-029
- BFF: Gracie Grape (Snow Cone)

I have ◯

OJ POP

- FLAVORSOME FACT: Wakey, wakey, it's time for OJ Pop. Her sunny personality is like a good squeeze . . . this Pop doesn't stop!
- CUTE QUOTE: "I never run out of juice. I always concentrate on getting things done."
- SCENT: Orange
- SERIES: 2
- CHARACTER NUMBER: 2-050
- BFF: Lemony Pop (Freezie Pop)

I have ◯

Fruit Nums

Get your five-a-day with these fantastically fit Nums. One sniff of their tangy flavors will have you begging for the fruit bowl.

I have ◯

Stew Tomato

- **FLAVORSOME FACT:** Stew Tomato is having an identity crisis. He knows he's a fruit, but he feels like a vegetable. If only life was puree and simple.
- **CUTE QUOTE:** "Who should I hang out with? Fruit salad or regular salad?"
- **SCENT:** Tomato
- **SERIES:** 3
- **CHARACTER NUMBER:** 3-024
- **BFF:** Victor Vines (Fruit)

Georgia Peach

- **FLAVORSOME FACT:** All the other Nums know that Georgia Peach is kind and generous. She makes sure that they all get a peach of the pie.
- **CUTE QUOTE:** "My memory is a little fuzzy at times. Um, what was I saying?"
- **SCENT:** Peach
- **SERIES:** 3
- **CHARACTER NUMBER:** 3-017
- **BFF:** Peachy Stamp-It (Nom)

I have ◯

I have ◯

Becky Banana

- 🍌 FLAVORSOME FACT: Cheerful Becky Banana just loves monkeying around. She enjoys hanging out and laughing with her friends, especially if it's a whole bunch of the other Nana Num Noms.
- 🍌 CUTE QUOTE: "Hey, guys, let's have some fun and slide down the banana-nister!"
- 🍌 SCENT: Banana
- 🍌 SERIES: 3
- 🍌 CHARACTER NUMBER: 3-021
- 🍌 BFF: Nana Erase-It (Nom)

Victor Vines

- 🍇 FLAVORSOME FACT: If you want to keep your secrets safe, remember not to tell Victor Vines. He just loves to gossip, and when he hears really juicy stuff he goes bright purple.
- 🍇 CUTE QUOTE: "Listen up, everyone! I heard this on the grapevine, so it must be true!"
- 🍇 SCENT: Grape
- 🍇 SERIES: 3
- 🍇 CHARACTER NUMBER: 3-018
- 🍇 BFF: Stew Tomato (Fruit)

I have ◯

Coco Cali

- FLAVORSOME FACT: Most of the time Coco Cali keeps it all together. But if she's stressed, she acts like a nut-case. And when she cracks, everything comes spilling out.
- CUTE QUOTE: "How dare you . . . that's sooo not true. You'd never catch me crying over spilled milk."
- SCENT: Coconut
- SERIES: 3
- CHARACTER NUMBER: 3-022
- BFF: Madelyn Mango (Gummy)

I have ◯

Ava Apple

- FLAVORSOME FACT: There is nothing rotten about crimson cutie Ava. All her Num Nom friends agree that she's the good apple that makes the bushel better.
- CUTE QUOTE: "Let's get to the core of the matter . . . I have never had worms!"
- SCENT: Red apple
- SERIES: 3
- CHARACTER NUMBER: 3-026
- BFF: Orange Sugar Gummy (Gummy)

Special EDITION

I have ◯

Zane Zest

- FLAVORSOME FACT: Sporty cheerleader Zane Zest just loves being in the lime-light. He's usually at the top of the pyramid because that's where he feels the most sub-lime. He doesn't want to be wedged in at the bottom.
- CUTE QUOTE: "Lime so glad to be here, folks."
- SCENT: Key lime
- SERIES: 3
- CHARACTER NUMBER: 3-016
- BFF: Cyrus Citrus (Fruit)

I have ◯

Sadie Seeds

- FLAVORSOME FACT: This happy Fruit thinks gardening is great fun. In fact, she really digs it. Sadie always likes to plant the seed of an idea to see what grows from it.
- CUTE QUOTE: "I make sure everything I grow is berry fresh . . . . I would never let it go to seed."
- SCENT: Strawberry
- SERIES: 3
- CHARACTER NUMBER: 3-023
- BFF: Melony Seeds (Fruit)

I have ◯

Piney Apple

FLAVORSOME FACT: Sweet little Piney Apple is such a fine-apple. So fine, in fact, that she insists on wearing a crown wherever she goes. If anyone wants to touch it, she tells them to leaf it alone.

CUTE QUOTE: "Know what? I'm so sweet, I've got a crush on myself."

SCENT: Pineapple

SERIES: 3

CHARACTER NUMBER: 3-019

BFF: Paula Pumpkin (Veggie)

I have ◯

Oscar Orange

FLAVORSOME FACT: Batten down the hatches! Raise the mainsail! Daring voyages on the high seas really make Oscar's juices flow. Well, he is a naval orange after all.

CUTE QUOTE: "Farewell, friends . . . I'll see you schooner or later."

SCENT: Orange

SERIES: 3

CHARACTER NUMBER: 3-015

BFFs: Slice and Wedge Erase-It (Noms)

I have ◯

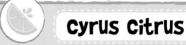

I have ◯

Cyrus Citrus

- **FLAVORSOME FACT:** This yellow fellow is Cyrus Citrus. His favorite pastime is playing sports with his Num Nom pals. He regularly wins, but if he's on the losing side, he's never sour about it.
- **CUTE QUOTE:** "It's all about taking part. Who would want to be a bitter lemon?"
- **SCENT:** Lemon
- **SERIES:** 3
- **CHARACTER NUMBER:** 3-025
- **BFF:** Zane Zest (Fruit)

Melony Seeds

- **FLAVORSOME FACT:** Melony knows how important it is to keep sowing the seeds of friendship. She's always nearby if her best friend is feeling melon-choly.
- **CUTE QUOTE:** "Whichever way you slice it, I just wanted to say thanks a melon for being my pal."
- **SCENT:** Watermelon
- **SERIES:** 3
- **CHARACTER NUMBER:** 3-020
- **BFF:** Sadie Seeds (Fruit)

I have ◯

Gummy Nums

Chew chew . . . all aboard the Gummy Express!
You're about to go on a journey to Gummy Town.
But watch out . . . it might get sticky at times.

I have ◯

Cherie Gummy

- FLAVORSOME FACT: Yes, cher-rie, this sweetie loves a good tale. She makes sure she hears the whole story . . . she never cherry-picks her facts!
- CUTE QUOTE: "I always chews to see the best in people!"
- SCENT: Cherry
- SERIES: Lights 1
- CHARACTER NUMBER: L-017
- BFF: Sparkle Berry Gummy (Gummy)

Glitter Berry

- FLAVORSOME FACT: Rise and shine, everyone! This stylish Num puts glitter on in the morning, so she shines all day.
- CUTE QUOTE: "When you're feeling blue, just add glitter!"
- SCENT: Blueberry
- SERIES: Lights 1
- CHARACTER NUMBER: L-020
- BFF: Blueberry Light-Up (Nom)

I have ◯

I have ◯

Bubble Gummy

- **FLAVORSOME FACT:** This Gummy came here to cause mischief and chew bubble gum . . . but she's all out of bubble gum. So watch out! Things might get blown up out of proportion. . . .
- **CUTE QUOTE:** "What's my favorite kind of music? Pop, of course!"
- **SCENT:** Bubblegum
- **SERIES:** Lights 1
- **CHARACTER NUMBER:** L-023
- **BFF:** Mintee Light-Up (Nom)

Piña Gummy

- **FLAVORSOME FACT:** Every day is a crazy hair day for pretty Piña Gummy! It keeps on curling and she can't do a thing with it What's the solution? Add a sweet little bow and smile, of course!
- **CUTE QUOTE:** "Some think I have a spiky personality, but I think I'm sweet!"
- **SCENT:** Pineapple
- **SERIES:** Lights 1
- **CHARACTER NUMBER:** L-013
- **BFF:** Kiwi Light-Up (Nom)

I have ◯

I have ◯

 Juicy Gummy

- FLAVORSOME FACT: Whoosh! Busy Juicy Gummy is always on the go. She is so full of energy she never runs out of juice. Everyone wants to know her secret scent. If only she would stay still long enough for someone to find out!
- CUTE QUOTE: "It's time to let loose the juice!"
- SCENT: Mystery
- SERIES: Lights 1
- CHARACTER NUMBER: L-018
- BFF: It's a mystery . . . .

Raz Sugar

- FLAVORSOME FACT: This Num dreads the winter. Whenever she gets a cold, it's really tricky to understand what she's saying. Her voice is just so raspy!
- CUTE QUOTE: "I'm going to stay berry quiet. If you can't hear me properly, I might end up in a jam!"
- SCENT: Raspberry
- SERIES: Lights 1
- CHARACTER NUMBER: L-021
- BFF: Raspberry Light-Up (Nom)

I have ◯

C.C. Sugar Gummy

- **FLAVORSOME FACT:** C.C. Sugar is little miss popular. And no wonder . . . she'll do anything for friends who have helped her out. She always sticks by those that love her.
- **CUTE QUOTE:** "I've got no complaints. I have a super-sweet life."
- **SCENT:** Cotton candy
- **SERIES:** Lights 1
- **CHARACTER NUMBER:** L-015
- **BFF:** Candy Sparkle Snow (Snow Cone)

I have ◯

Grape Gummy

- **FLAVORSOME FACT:** Caring Grape Gummy is a real mommy's girl. Every day she tells her mom, "You did a grape job raisin' me." She often visits other Grape Num Noms because they like to hang around in bunches.
- **CUTE QUOTE:** "Hope you have a grape day!"
- **SCENT:** Grape
- **SERIES:** Lights 1
- **CHARACTER NUMBER:** L-024
- **BFF:** Grape Light-Up (Nom)

Special **EDITION**

I have ◯

Sparkle Berry Gummy

- **FLAVORSOME FACT:** This gleeful Gummy has a sweet personality. She really is berry nice to everyone she meets! And she likes to think she brings a bit of glitz into their lives.
- **CUTE QUOTE:** "I think a cool drink always tastes better through a straw."
- **SCENT:** Strawberry
- **SERIES:** Lights 1
- **CHARACTER NUMBER:** L-014
- **BFF:** Cherie Gummy (Gummy)

I have ◯

Madelyn Mango

- **FLAVORSOME FACT:** Fun-loving Madelyn Mango loves a good laugh and is always full of silly puns. Once she gets started, she s-talks and s-talks for hours!
- **CUTE QUOTE:** "Nearly all my jokes start 'A man-goes into a smoothie bar . . .' Fruit funnies are the best!"
- **SCENT:** Mango
- **SERIES:** Lights 1
- **CHARACTER NUMBER:** L-019
- **BFF:** Coco Cali (Fruit)

I have ◯

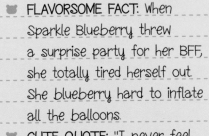

Sparkle BlueBerry

- **FLAVORSOME FACT:** When Sparkle Blueberry threw a surprise party for her BFF, she totally tired herself out. She blueberry hard to inflate all the balloons.
- **CUTE QUOTE:** "I never feel blue. I think it's because of my sparkling personality!"
- **SCENT:** Wildberry
- **SERIES:** Lights 1
- **CHARACTER NUMBER:** L-022
- **BFF:** Blue Razz Pop (Freezie Pop)

I have ◯

Orange Sugar Gummy

- **FLAVORSOME FACT:** This juicy little Num always gets good grades at school. Why? Because she knows it pays to concentrate! She carries her books between lessons using a cart-on wheels.
- **CUTE QUOTE:** "Orange you glad you listened to the teacher like me?"
- **SCENT:** Orange
- **SERIES:** Lights 1
- **CHARACTER NUMBER:** L-016
- **BFF:** Ava Apple (Fruit)

I have ◯

Ice Cream Nums

You scream! I scream!
We all scream for ice cream!
Get a scoopful of these cool dudes. . . .

I have ◯

Nilla Twirl

- FLAVORSOME FACT: Nilla Twirl must be a candidate for the cutest Num in town. She's so sweet, she has hopped into everyone's hearts.
- CUTE QUOTE: "My sweet smile will have you in a twirl!"
- SCENT: Vanilla
- SERIES: 1
- CHARACTER NUMBER: 125
- BFF: Choco Go-Go (Nom)

Lemony Cream

- FLAVORSOME FACT: This cool dude is super-good at everything he tries. When given a challenge, he proves that he's the cream of the crop!
- CUTE QUOTE: "No problem . . . that's easy peasy, lemon squeezy!"
- SCENT: Lemon
- SERIES: 1
- CHARACTER NUMBER: 132
- BFF: Berry Scoop (Ice Cream)

I have ◯

Van Minty

- **FLAVORSOME FACT:** No doubt about it, Van Minty is one of the coolest Nums in the kitchen. Just one look from him and you'll melt. He always tries to look after himself because it's important to stay in mint condition.
- **CUTE QUOTE:** "Until next time, stay cool"
- **SCENT:** Mint
- **SERIES:** 1
- **CHARACTER NUMBER:** 141
- **BFF:** Nilla Gloss-Up (Nom)

I have ◯

Cherry Chip

- **FLAVORSOME FACT:** This red-faced guy may seem like he's got a chip on his shoulder, so the other Num Noms worry about making him angry. But underneath it all, he's cherry nice and always helps when the chips are down.
- **CUTE QUOTE:** "Another bite of the cherry, anyone?"
- **SCENT:** Cherry
- **SERIES:** 1
- **CHARACTER NUMBER:** 137
- **BFF:** Razzberry Go-Go (Nom)

I have ◯

Berry Twirl

I have ◯

- **FLAVORSOME FACT:** This little twirly is famous for being a real chatterbox. She can go on and on till she's blue in the face.
- **CUTE QUOTE:** "What's that? Me, a chatterbox? Really? No, I don't think so. Who said that? I mean, I like to talk, but who doesn't? I'm just the friendly type, is all . . ."
- **SCENT:** Blueberry
- **SERIES:** 2
- **CHARACTER NUMBER:** 2-058
- **BFF:** Cherry Gummy Stamp-It (Nom)

Billy Banana

- **FLAVORSOME FACT:** Billy thinks if you hang around in one place for too long, you start going soft. So if you see him, don't let this guy slip away, 'cause he's likely to split!
- **CUTE QUOTE:** "Hey, guys . . . chill out"
- **SCENT:** Banana
- **SERIES:** 1
- **CHARACTER NUMBER:** 128
- **BFF:** Nana Cream (Cupcake)

I have ◯

Parker Peach

- FLAVORSOME FACT: Parker is one chilled-out Num. At first he might seem a bit dopey, but give Peach a chance and you'll find he makes everything better.
- CUTE QUOTE: "Life's a peach, man."
- SCENT: Peach
- SERIES: 2
- CHARACTER NUMBER: 2-055
- BFF: Icy Peach Go-Go (Nom)

I have ◯

StrawBerry SPrinkles

- FLAVORSOME FACT: If you're feeling down, you need Strawberry Sprinkles! This cheerful character spreads strawberry-flavored happiness wherever she goes.
- CUTE QUOTE: "Always sprinkle joy!"
- SCENT: Strawberry
- SERIES: 1
- CHARACTER NUMBER: 135
- BFF: Cherry Gloss-Up (Nom)

I have ◯

ChoCo Cream

- FLAVORSOME FACT: Being fabulous is a must for Choco; his pink swirl must always be perfect. That's why he's nicknamed 'Choco Cream-boat'.
- CUTE QUOTE: "Seven days without Choco makes one weak."
- SCENT: Chocolate
- SERIES: 1
- CHARACTER NUMBER: 142
- BFF: Strawberry Go-Go (Nom)

I have ◯

Pepper Minty Shine

- **FLAVORSOME FACT:** Pretty Pepper Minty Shine is quite shy and usually keeps to herself. But she always shows up when winter comes around . . . the holidays make her feel all scent-i-mint-al!
- **CUTE QUOTE:** "Wintertime is when I shine!"
- **SCENT:** Peppermint
- **SERIES:** 2
- **CHARACTER NUMBER:** 2-061
- **BFF:** Pumpkin Spice (Ice Cream)

I have ◯

Berry Scoop

- **FLAVORSOME FACT:** Mmm-hmm! This little Ice Cream Num sure looks good! With his waffly cute ears, he's berry cool. He wants to become a reporter because he knows he'll get all the best scoops.
- **CUTE QUOTE:** "It's berry nice to meet you."
- **SCENT:** Blueberry
- **SERIES:** 1
- **CHARACTER NUMBER:** 138
- **BFF:** Lemony Cream (Ice Cream)

I have ◯

I have ◯

Connie Confetti

- **FLAVORSOME FACT:** If you want your birthday party to go with a bang, then this is the Num Nom to call. Connie just loves surprises. It's just as well .... there's an explosion of confetti wherever she goes!
- **CUTE QUOTE:** "Surprise, surprise, everybody! It's me!"
- **SCENT:** Birthday cake
- **SERIES:** 1
- **CHARACTER NUMBER:** 144
- **BFF:** Everyone!

B.B. Scoops

- **FLAVORSOME FACT:** This cool guy has music in his soul, but his tastes aren't too varied. He's a huge fan of R and B.B., but his favorite kind of music just has to be classic blues.
- **CUTE QUOTE:** "Ba-ba-do-bah! You've got me singin' the blues, sweetheart"
- **SCENT:** Blueberry
- **SERIES:** 2
- **CHARACTER NUMBER:** 2-118
- **BFF:** Berry Crème Gloss-Up (Nom)

I have ◯

Orange Cream

- **FLAVORSOME FACT:** Orange Cream fills her time visiting all of her special friends. But don't worry, she'll make sure she saves a section of her day just for you.
- **CUTE QUOTE:** "Don't be bitter; be sweet"
- **SCENT:** Orange
- **SERIES:** 1
- **CHARACTER NUMBER:** 146
- **BFF:** Nilla Go-Go (Nom)

Special **EDITION**

I have ◯

Lisa Lemon

- **FLAVORSOME FACT:** Lisa Lemon looks on the bright side. Her positive outlook makes her great company . . . she's never a sourpuss!
- **CUTE QUOTE:** "If life gives you lemons, lucky you! Lemons are great!"
- **SCENT:** Lemon
- **SERIES:** 1
- **CHARACTER NUMBER:** 131
- **BFF:** Piña Gloss-Up (Nom)

I have ◯

Mint Twirl

- **FLAVORSOME FACT:** Mint Twirl loves nothing more than watching a good film. Her favorite films are ro-mint-ic comedies.
- **CUTE QUOTE:** "A movie triple feature? Now that's what I call entertain-mint!"
- **SCENT:** Mint
- **SERIES:** 2
- **CHARACTER NUMBER:** 2-059
- **BFF:** Blueberry Jelly (Jelly Bean)

I have ◯

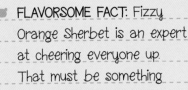

I have ◯

Peachy Cream

- FLAVORSOME FACT: Sweet-smelling Peachy is a happy bunny. She always has a warm, fuzzy feeling all over! She doesn't take things for granted. She ap-peach-iates all of her friends.
- CUTE QUOTE: "I'm just peachy. Thanks for asking!"
- SCENT: Peach
- SERIES: 1
- CHARACTER NUMBER: 130
- BFF: Raspberry Cream (Cupcake)

Orange Sherbet

- FLAVORSOME FACT: Fizzy Orange Sherbet is an expert at cheering everyone up. That must be something to do with her effervescent personality! She sher is fun to have around!
- CUTE QUOTE: "You look like you need a hug. Come on, give me a squeeze."
- SCENT: Orange
- SERIES: 1
- CHARACTER NUMBER: 133
- BFF: Orange Twirl (Ice Cream)

I have ◯

I have ◯

Neo Trio

- **FLAVORSOME FACT:** Say "Ciao" to friendly Neo Trio. This Num loves everything Italian, including the art, the cars, the fashion . . . and the gelato. His ideal vacation would be Rome-ing around, taking in a pizza the action.
- **CUTE QUOTE:** "Better chocoLATE than never!"
- **SCENT:** Chocolate
- **SERIES:** 1
- **CHARACTER NUMBER:** 145
- **BFF:** Mimi Mango (Cupcake)

Bailey Bubblegum

- **FLAVORSOME FACT:** Super-cute Bailey is as sweet as candy. In fact, she's so adorable you'll want to chew her up! She's saving up for a day trip with the other Bubblegum Num Noms . . . they're going to take the chew chew train!
- **CUTE QUOTE:** "On your marks, get set, blow a bubble!"
- **SCENT:** Bubblegum
- **SERIES:** 1
- **CHARACTER NUMBER:** 139
- **BFF:** Orange Swirl (Cupcake)

I have ◯

Nana Splits

- **FLAVORSOME FACT:** Some days, Nana Splits likes to get a little crazy. But she really goes nuts with the Ice Cream Nums on Sundaes. That's why she doesn't travel on weekends . . . she doesn't want to be a-wafer so long.
- **CUTE QUOTE:** "Woo-hoo! Let's go bananas!"
- **SCENT:** Banana
- **SERIES:** 2
- **CHARACTER NUMBER:** 2-056
- **BFF:** Peanut Go-Go (Nom)

I have ◯

Tango Mango

- **FLAVORSOME FACT:** This Num just loves to dance. It doesn't matter what music is playing, though. It could be pop, rock, disco, rap, or classical . . . he always dances the tango. Everyone has one word for this Mango . . . tree-mendous!
- **CUTE QUOTE:** "This man-goes crazy for tango."
- **SCENT:** Mango
- **SERIES:** 1
- **CHARACTER NUMBER:** 129
- **BFF:** Banana Go-Go (Nom)

I have ◯

caramel cream

- **FLAVORSOME FACT:** Some of the other Num Noms might say that Caramel Cream is cold, but with her warm topping, she's bound to melt your heart. It's easy to get stuck on her.
- **CUTE QUOTE:** "Yawn! Is it bedtime already? Sweet creams, everybody!"
- **SCENT:** Caramel
- **SERIES:** 1
- **CHARACTER NUMBER:** 126
- **BFF:** Nana Berry (Ice Cream)

I have ◯

Cherry Scoop

- **FLAVORSOME FACT:** This nosy little Num loves nothing more than gossiping with his buddies. He's always looking for a good scoop. He's a very good driver, although he doesn't like rocky roads.
- **CUTE QUOTE:** "Don't clam up. You know cherry well that I can keep a secret!"
- **SCENT:** Cherry
- **SERIES:** 2
- **CHARACTER NUMBER:** 2-060
- **BFF:** Cola Gloss-Up (Nom)

Special **EDITION**

I have ◯

Orange Twirl

- FLAVORSOME FACT: Orange Twirl can find it hard to make friends. She's just too tangy for some! But if you get to know her she'll be the best BFF you could ask for.
- CUTE QUOTE: "I'm a twirly girly!"
- SCENT: Orange
- SERIES: 1
- CHARACTER NUMBER: 134
- BFF: Orange Sherbet (Ice Cream)

I have ◯

Choco Nilla

- FLAVORSOME FACT: If you hear strange noises in the middle of the night, don't worry. It's sure to be Choco Nilla having a midnight feast.
- CUTE QUOTE: "Nighttime is the right time for Num Noms fun and games."
- SCENT: Chocolate
- SERIES: 1
- CHARACTER NUMBER: 143
- BFF: Caramelly Go-Go (Nom)

I have ◯

Minty Chip

- FLAVORSOME FACT: This fresh-faced fella is Minty Chip. His friends love that he's always upbeat and full of excite-mint.
- CUTE QUOTE: "When the chips are down, I'm here to help."
- SCENT: Mint
- SERIES: 1
- CHARACTER NUMBER: 140
- BFF: Minty Swirl (Cupcake)

I have ◯

Nana Berry

- FLAVORSOME FACT: This Num loves to play funny tricks on her friends. When it comes to pulling pranks, she's the best of the bunch.
- CUTE QUOTE: "I wonder who left that banana skin lying around . . . ha ha!"
- SCENT: Banana
- SERIES: 1
- CHARACTER NUMBER: 127
- BFF: Caramel Cream (Ice Cream)

I have ◯

Pumpkin Spice

- FLAVORSOME FACT: This Num will certainly spice up your day with his funny jokes. He's such a great comedian that all the other Num Noms call him the "Pun King" Geddit?
- CUTE QUOTE: "How do you fix a broken pumpkin? With a pumpkin patch!"
- SCENT: Pumpkin Spice
- SERIES: 2
- CHARACTER NUMBER: 2-062
- BFF: Pepper Minty Shine (Ice Cream)

Special EDITION

I have ◯

Lulu Licorice

- **FLAVORSOME FACT:** Perky Lulu Licorice is not to everyone's taste. She does end up in all sorts of trouble. But when you get to know her, she's confident that you'll think she has anise flavor.
- **CUTE QUOTE:** "I may have come from the sticks, but now I'm a lico-rich girl!"
- **SCENT:** Licorice
- **SERIES:** 1
- **CHARACTER NUMBER:** 124
- **BFF:** Cheery Cherie (Cupcake)

I have ◯

Sara Strawberry

- **FLAVORSOME FACT:** This Num is fantastic at organizing events. From bake sales to movie nights, when Sara gets the seed of an idea, everyone has a field day. She keeps one eye open to stay on top of everything.
- **CUTE QUOTE:** "My plans always come to fruit-ition."
- **SCENT:** Strawberry
- **SERIES:** 2
- **CHARACTER NUMBER:** 2-057
- **BFF:** Pickly Go-Go (Nom)

I have ◯

I have ◯

Sherry Berry

- **FLAVORSOME FACT:** Lovely Sherry Berry is a laid-back little lady. She manages to keep her cool . . . even when she gets in a jam. It's no wonder the other Num Noms are always lining up to cone-gratulate her!
- **CUTE QUOTE:** "Do you wanna chill with me?"
- **SCENT:** Strawberry
- **SERIES:** 1
- **CHARACTER NUMBER:** 136
- **BFF:** Orange Gloss-Up (Nom)

Mint T. Cream

- **FLAVORSOME FACT:** This cute little kitty smells as good as she looks. In fact, she is ex-cream-ely cool. She'd love to be an astronaut in the future . . . . a float in space sounds like a great idea.
- **CUTE QUOTE:** "Studying is smart. I learned all I know in ele-mint-ary school."
- **SCENT:** Mint
- **SERIES:** 2
- **CHARACTER NUMBER:** 2-119
- **BFF:** Mint Crème Gloss-Up (Nom)

Special **EDITION**

I have ◯

Jelly Bean Nums

These sweet little Num Noms are full of beans. They just can't stop jumping for joy!

I have ◯

RaspBerry Jelly

- **FLAVORSOME FACT:** Raspberry Jelly has tons of experience. She has bean to so many different places that nothing surprises her anymore.
- **CUTE QUOTE:** "My motto is bean there, done that"
- **SCENT:** Raspberry
- **SERIES:** 2
- **CHARACTER NUMBER:** 2-076
- **BFF:** Butterscotch Go-Go (Nom)

BuBBly Jelly

- **FLAVORSOME FACT:** She may look grouchy, but it's because Bubbly has a lot on her mind. She's a multitasker ... she can go for a walk AND chew bubblegum at the same time.
- **CUTE QUOTE:** "I'm busy and bubbly"
- **SCENT:** Bubblegum
- **SERIES:** 2
- **CHARACTER NUMBER:** 2-079
- **BFF:** Bubbly Gloss-Up (Nom)

I have ◯

I have ◯

Kiwi Jelly

- 🍬 FLAVORSOME FACT: If you think that you're looking at a high-class Num, then you're right. Kiwi Jelly has royalty in her family. She owns the kiwi to the kingdom!
- 🍬 CUTE QUOTE: "Make way for a real Jelly Bean queen on the scene!"
- 🍬 SCENT: Kiwi
- 🍬 SERIES: 2
- 🍬 CHARACTER NUMBER: 2-073
- 🍬 BFF: Strawberry Pop (Freezie Pop)

Mallow Jelly

- 🍬 FLAVORSOME FACT: All the Num Noms like to gossip to Mallow Jelly. Everyone is happy to share their secrets with her because she never spills the beans. She often likes to stay at home where it's warm and toasty.
- 🍬 CUTE QUOTE: "Hey, I know what you mean, Jelly Bean!"
- 🍬 SCENT: Marshmallow
- 🍬 SERIES: 2
- 🍬 CHARACTER NUMBER: 2-081
- 🍬 BFF: S'mores Gloss-Up (Nom)

Special **EDITION**

I have ◯

Orange Jelly

- FLAVORSOME FACT: Poor Orange Jelly has put so much effort into making friends she looks worn out. It's a shame because when there's any juicy gossip around, she just can't concentrate!
- CUTE QUOTE: "Don't listen; that's just beans-talk!"
- SCENT: Orange
- SERIES: 2
- CHARACTER NUMBER: 2-074
- BFF: Cream Berry Jelly (Jelly Bean)

I have 〇

Confetti Jelly

- FLAVORSOME FACT: Confetti is always happy, no matter what life throws at her. Whenever there is a party or a celebration being planned, she has always bean at the top of the guest list. 'Tis the season to be jelly!
- CUTE QUOTE: "Variety is what makes life sweet"
- SCENT: Birthday cake
- SERIES: 2
- CHARACTER NUMBER: 2-080
- BFF: Pinky Puffs (Fair Food)

I have 〇

Grape Jelly

- FLAVORSOME FACT: Whoa! This Num looks real grumpy, but don't worry ... she actually goes to grape lengths to help others.
- CUTE QUOTE: "Be warned ... with grape power comes grape responsibility."
- SCENT: Grape
- SERIES: 2
- CHARACTER NUMBER: 2-078
- BFF: Grape Soda Pop (Freezie Pop)

I have ◯

Piña Jelly

- FLAVORSOME FACT: It's true that looks can be deceiving. Piña Jelly may be prickly on the outside, but on the inside she's as sweet as pineapple pie.
- CUTE QUOTE: "I'm pining for my BFF!"
- SCENT: Pineapple
- SERIES: 2
- CHARACTER NUMBER: 2-072
- BFF: Piña Aloha (Pizza)

I have ◯

Cream Berry Jelly

- FLAVORSOME FACT: Cream Berry Jelly has bean nicknamed the bean counter because she never wants her friends to get lost.
- CUTE QUOTE: " ... four Jelly Beans, five Jelly Beans, six Jelly Beans, ZZZZZZ ... "
- SCENT: Strawberry
- SERIES: 2
- CHARACTER NUMBER: 2-075
- BFF: Orange Jelly (Jelly Bean)

I have ◯

I have ◯

BlueBerry Jelly

- **FLAVORSOME FACT:** Are you feeling sad? Then why not spend some time with cheerful Blueberry Jelly? With a wink and a smile, she'll blow your blues away and you'll soon start feeling berry good.
- **CUTE QUOTE:** "I'm one popular jelly . . . folks just love bean with me!"
- **SCENT:** Blueberry
- **SERIES:** 2
- **CHARACTER NUMBER:** 2-077
- **BFF:** Mint Twirl (Ice Cream)

Cotton Jelly

- **FLAVORSOME FACT:** Bouncy Cotton Jelly isn't the brightest Num in the pack. You could say that she doesn't know beans . . . or much else! But when you're as sweet as she is, it doesn't matter.
- **CUTE QUOTE:** "I'm feeling blue, but I'm in the pink, too!"
- **SCENT:** Cotton candy
- **SERIES:** 2
- **CHARACTER NUMBER:** 2-125
- **BFF:** Candy Crème Gloss-Up (Nom)

Special **EDITION**

I have ◯

Marshmallow Nums

Go easy on these little sweeties. They have soft centers and they don't like dangerous activities. They only play softball.

I have ◯

Toasty Mallow

- **FLAVORSOME FACT:** Toasty Mallow's head is often lost in big, fluffy clouds. Her favorite daydream? A great evening by the campfire.
- **CUTE QUOTE:** "Some like it hot I like it toasted."
- **SCENT:** Toasted marshmallow
- **SERIES:** 3
- **CHARACTER NUMBER:** 3-036
- **BFF:** Cory Custard (Donut)

Rachel Raspberry

- **FLAVORSOME FACT:** The other Nums look up to Rachel Raspberry because she's a born leader. She sure makes some sweet decisions.
- **CUTE QUOTE:** "I know my own mind berry well."
- **SCENT:** Raspberry
- **SERIES:** 3
- **CHARACTER NUMBER:** 3-043
- **BFF:** Choco-Razz Gloss-Up (Nom)

I have ◯

I have ◯

Minty Mallow

- FLAVORSOME FACT: Upbeat Minty Mallow is a "glass half full" kind of Num. This positive Marshmallow always believes that whatever is mint to be, will be.
- CUTE QUOTE: "It doesn't cost you anything to pay someone a compli-mint"
- SCENT: Mint
- SERIES: 3
- CHARACTER NUMBER: 3-034
- BFF: Peyton Peppermint (Candy)

Blue Barry

- FLAVORSOME FACT: Wherever he goes, Blue Barry is sparkling company. Everyone loves him because he's such a softie. He's just sooo squishy . . . inside and out!
- CUTE QUOTE: "Sometimes plans go wrong. You gotta take the rough with the soft"
- SCENT: Blue raspberry
- SERIES: 3
- CHARACTER NUMBER: 3-046
- BFF: Strawberry Snow (Snow Cone)

Special **EDITION**

I have ◯

C.C. Candy

- **FLAVORSOME FACT:** C.C. Candy thinks life is just dandy! This confident Num usually keeps to herself. But if her BFF Bella Bubblegum is in trouble, she will show her true stripes . . . seriously sweet!
- **CUTE QUOTE:** "Now just a cotton-pickin' minute!"
- **SCENT:** Cotton candy
- **SERIES:** 3
- **CHARACTER NUMBER:** 3-039
- **BFF:** Bella Bubblegum (Marshmallow)

I have ◯

Softy Mallow

- **FLAVORSOME FACT:** Summer is the perfect season for Softy Mallow. She loves the sunshine. For her, nothing makes a warm day more special than taking a quick dip . . . in chocolate!
- **CUTE QUOTE:** "Do you want to know a secret? I have a real soft spot for you."
- **SCENT:** Marshmallow
- **SERIES:** 3
- **CHARACTER NUMBER:** 3-041
- **BFF:** Powdered Sugars (Donut)

I have ◯

StrawBerry Mallow

- **FLAVORSOME FACT:** Strawberry Mallow often gets herself in a jam because she's forever falling asleep. But at least while she's dozing she's having sweet dreams.
- **CUTE QUOTE:** "I wish you a berry goodnight"
- **SCENT:** Strawberry
- **SERIES:** 3
- **CHARACTER NUMBER:** 3-042
- **BFF:** Sugar Stripes (Candy)

I have ◯

Sugar Nana

- **FLAVORSOME FACT:** Ask any of the Num Noms who the worst driver is and they'll all say it's Sugar Nana. This yellow mallow is always peeling out of the driveway.
- **CUTE QUOTE:** "I like to give my friends the slip"
- **SCENT:** Banana
- **SERIES:** 3
- **CHARACTER NUMBER:** 3-044
- **BFF:** Straw-Nana Gloss-Up (Nom)

I have ◯

Bella BuBBlegum

- **FLAVORSOME FACT:** Surprise, surprise . . . it's Bella Bubblegum! This Num must have racing stripes because she always pops up in the most unexpected places.
- **CUTE QUOTE:** "I'm no bubble-head."
- **SCENT:** Bubblegum
- **SERIES:** 3
- **CHARACTER NUMBER:** 3-038
- **BFF:** C.C. Candy (Marshmallow)

I have ◯

Sara S'mores

🍬 FLAVORSOME FACT: The first in line for the annual Num Noms campout is always Sara S'mores. This little firecracker enjoys the campfire singing the most. The lively tunes just make her melt.

🍬 CUTE QUOTE: "Music makes me go all gooey inside."

🍬 SCENT: S'mores

🍬 SERIES: 3

🍬 CHARACTER NUMBER: 3-037

🍬 BFF: Mallow Erase-It (Nom)

B. Berry Mallow

🍬 FLAVORSOME FACT: Shhh! Can you hear soft footsteps? Watch out . . . B. Berry Mallow likes to surprise her friends by jumping out at them. After all, this little trickster is a boo berry.

🍬 CUTE QUOTE: "Wanna hear a scary story? Don't worry, nobody meets a sticky end."

🍬 SCENT: Blueberry

🍬 SERIES: 3

🍬 CHARACTER NUMBER: 3-035

🍬 BFF: Mintberry Gloss-Up (Nom)

I have ◯

Marsha Violet

FLAVORSOME FACT: All Num Noms like to go a little crazy sometimes. But things tend to get berry wild when this special lady shows up.

CUTE QUOTE: "You'd better tread softly around me"

SCENT: Wildberry

SERIES: 3

CHARACTER NUMBER: 3-045

BFF: Crystal W. Berry (Candy)

Special **EDITION**

I have ◯

Maya Mallow

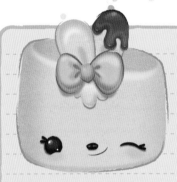

FLAVORSOME FACT: It's totally impossible to ignore Maya Mallow. Whether it's the s'mores or the cereal bowl, she always has to be the center of attention.

CUTE QUOTE: "May-a sit here, please?"

SCENT: Sweet marshmallow

SERIES: 3

CHARACTER NUMBER: 3-033

BFF: Emma Eggplant (Veggie)

I have ◯

Cocoa Mallow

FLAVORSOME FACT: If you're feeling stressed, Cocoa has some suggestions to help you mallow out. She knows that everything is much better when it's covered in chocolate.

CUTE QUOTE: "Chocolate is the best, bar none!"

SCENT: Chocolate

SERIES: 3

CHARACTER NUMBER: 3-040

BFF: Choco S'mores Gloss-Up (Nom)

I have ◯

Pizza Nums

One of these six Num Noms is sure to steal a pizza your heart! When it comes to fun, these guys always deliver.

Special EDITION

I have ◯

Margo Rita

- FLAVORSOME FACT: Margo Rita likes to keep things simple, which is why everyone loves her. She's so special, she just can't be topped!
- CUTE QUOTE: "I feel good from my head to-ma-toes"
- SCENT: Tomato
- SERIES: 2
- CHARACTER NUMBER: 2-016
- BFF: Haley Hot Dog (Diner Food)

Piña Aloha

- FLAVORSOME FACT: Bring on the flower power! Once Piña Aloha starts dancing, she can't stop, especially if she's listening to some cheesy tunes.
- CUTE QUOTE: "When everyone looks at me, I just have to ham it up"
- SCENT: Pineapple
- SERIES: 2
- CHARACTER NUMBER: 2-012
- BFF: Piña Jelly (Jelly Bean)

I have ◯

I have ◯

Peppy Roni

🐻 **FLAVORSOME FACT:** Want a quiet life? Then you better stay out of this Num's way if he's in a bad mood, because Peppy Roni sure has one fiery temper. If you bug him, he'll definitely give you a pizza his mind!

🐻 **CUTE QUOTE:** "Hey! Don't get saucy with me."

🐻 **SCENT:** Cheese

🐻 **SERIES:** 2

🐻 **CHARACTER NUMBER:** 2-011

🐻 **BFF:** Phili Roll (Sushi)

veggie Terry

🐻 **FLAVORSOME FACT:** Yawn! Veggie Terry is one sleepy PiZZZZZa Num. After a hard day, he prefers to order in and veg out. He's got a tiny bedroom, though . . . there's not mushroom in there.

🐻 **CUTE QUOTE:** "I think pepper-only is way better than pepperoni!"

🐻 **SCENT:** Cheese

🐻 **SERIES:** 2

🐻 **CHARACTER NUMBER:** 2-013

🐻 **BFF:** Cali Roll (Sushi)

I have ◯

I have ◯

Mozza Rella

- **FLAVORSOME FACT:** Cheesy Mozza Rella thinks she's a real funny gal Unfortunately, her jokes don't always hit the spot . . . they grate on her friends after a while!
- **CUTE QUOTE:** "There's no TOPPING my one-liners is there, guys? Uh, guys?"
- **SCENT:** Cheese
- **SERIES:** 2
- **CHARACTER NUMBER:** 2-014
- **BFF:** Berry Cheesecake (Cupcake)

Sammy S'mores

- **FLAVORSOME FACT:** As the only sweet-scented Pizza Num in the box, Sammy S'mores is a real individual It doesn't take much to get Sammy fired up, but everyone still goes crackers over him!
- **CUTE QUOTE:** "Don't overdo it! I never bite off s'more than I can chew!"
- **SCENT:** S'mores
- **SERIES:** 2
- **CHARACTER NUMBER:** 2-015
- **BFF:** Cara Mellie (Fair Food)

I have ◯

Snow Cone Nums

Time to meet the cutest cones in town.
Give it up for these frosty friends . . .
they're experts in snow business!

I have ◯

Triple Berry Icy

🍇 FLAVORSOME FACT: Triple Berry Icy sure is a wild child. But she's walking on berry thin ice . . . if she goes too far, she may have a meltdown.

🍇 CUTE QUOTE: "Come on, I got snow time for this."

🍇 SCENT: Wildberry

🍇 SERIES: Lights 1

🍇 CHARACTER NUMBER: L-006

🍇 BFF: Blueberry Stamp-It (Nom)

Candy Sparkle Snow

🍦 FLAVORSOME FACT: Whenever this Num snows up, there's a flurry of excitement. But if her pals get hot under the cone, Candy Sparkle helps them to chill out.

🍦 CUTE QUOTE: "I can be such a flake!"

🍦 SCENT: Cotton candy

🍦 SERIES: Lights 1

🍦 CHARACTER NUMBER: L-007

🍦 BFF: C.C. Sugar Gummy (Gummy)

I have ◯

I have ◯

Nea Snow

- **FLAVORSOME FACT:** The first time you meet Nea Snow, you might think she appears a bit frosty. But it's snow problem. She just needs to spend time with someone before she thaws out.
- **CUTE QUOTE:** "Don't be sad . . . I didn't mean to give you the cold shoulder."
- **SCENT:** Chocolate
- **SERIES:** Lights 1
- **CHARACTER NUMBER:** L-009
- **BFF:** Berry Light-Up (Nom)

Peachy Icy

- **FLAVORSOME FACT:** At first, Peachy Icy doesn't seem to be a chatterbox. But once you get to snow her, you'll discover that this Num believes in freeze-peach and just-ice for all.
- **CUTE QUOTE:** "Let's talk later. I don't want to put this conversation on ice."
- **SCENT:** Peach
- **SERIES:** Lights 1
- **CHARACTER NUMBER:** L-003
- **BFF:** Peachy Light-Up (Nom)

I have ◯

Apple Icy

- FLAVORSOME FACT: Apple Icy is snow-torious among her friends for her honest and snow-nonsense attitude. Silly games and tricks make her give you a cold stare.
- CUTE QUOTE: "Keep your ice peeled!"
- SCENT: Caramel apple
- SERIES: Lights 1
- CHARACTER NUMBER: L-008
- BFF: Grapple Gloss-Up (Nom)

I have ◯

Chloe Cola

- FLAVORSOME FACT: Despite her bubbly personality, Chloe Cola hates giving public speeches. She always freezes up.
- CUTE QUOTE: "I'm better at sparkling conversation, if you catch my drift."
- SCENT: Cola soda
- SERIES: Lights 1
- CHARACTER NUMBER: L-001
- BFF: Cherry Vanilla Gloss-Up (Nom)

I have ◯

StrawBerry Snow

- FLAVORSOME FACT: Strawberry Snow loves every winter sport going, except for ski jumping. It makes her break out in a cold sweat.
- CUTE QUOTE: "There's so much to do . . . I'm completely snowed under."
- SCENT: Strawberry
- SERIES: Lights 1
- CHARACTER NUMBER: L-012
- BFF: Blue Barry (Marshmallow)

Special **EDITION**

I have ◯

Lemonade Icy

- **FLAVORSOME FACT:** Giggly Lemonade Icy loves scaring friends by telling them tall tales. Her stories chill them to the bone. Luckily, they're not bitter about it.
- **CUTE QUOTE:** "If I was a breakfast cereal, I'd be Frosted Flakes!"
- **SCENT:** Sour lemon
- **SERIES:** Lights 1
- **CHARACTER NUMBER:** L-005
- **BFF:** Key Lime Icy (Snow Cone)

I have ◯

Trio Glow Cone ?

Special **EDITION**

- **FLAVORSOME FACT:** Talented Trio Glow Cone is all chill. He's so popular that whenever he shows up, his friends sing, "Freeze a Jolly Good Fellow" and he glows with pride.
- **CUTE QUOTE:** "It's important to stop in the middle of the day. Always make sure you ava-lanche break!"
- **SCENT:** Mystery
- **SERIES:** Lights 1
- **CHARACTER NUMBER:** L-010
- **BFF:** Mac Minty (Donut)

I have ◯

Key Lime Icy

🐻 FLAVORSOME FACT: Key Lime loves being with her BFF. She always gets a chill up her spine. Well, they do hang out in freezers, after all.

🐻 CUTE QUOTE: "I-cicle around to my friend's house every day."

🐻 SCENT: Key lime

🐻 SERIES: Lights 1

🐻 CHARACTER NUMBER: L-004

🐻 BFF: Lemonade Icy (Snow Cone)

I have ◯

Bubblegum Slushy

🐻 FLAVORSOME FACT: This Num loves school. 'Snow wonder . . . the day starts with Snow and Tell, and then a game of freeze tag at recess.

🐻 CUTE QUOTE: "After school I chillax by reading slushy stories."

🐻 SCENT: Bubblegum

🐻 SERIES: Lights 1

🐻 CHARACTER NUMBER: L-011

🐻 BFF: Bubbly Light-Up (Nom)

Special **EDITION**

I have ◯

Gracie Grape

🐻 FLAVORSOME FACT: Gracie is grape at debating. She begins by breaking the ice with a joke about ice picks. Then she keeps raisin' her game.

🐻 CUTE QUOTE: "When I've done a good job I-cing for joy."

🐻 SCENT: Grape

🐻 SERIES: Lights 1

🐻 CHARACTER NUMBER: L-002

🐻 BFF: Grape Freezie (Freezie Pop)

I have ◯

SUSHI NUMS

Nothing like one of the Sushi Nums to spice up your life. They know how to roll and smell soy delicious!

I have ◯

Tori Toro

- **FLAVORSOME FACT:** It's easy to tuna in to Tori Toro's wicked sense of humor! Her jokes reel the other Num Noms in and soon they're hooked!
- **CUTE QUOTE:** "I'm not going to fish for compliments."
- **SCENT:** Ginger
- **SERIES:** 2
- **CHARACTER NUMBER:** 2-018
- **BFF:** Lemon Gummy Stamp-It (Nom)

Ami Avocado

- **FLAVORSOME FACT:** Ami sometimes finds it hard to keep her cool. If she gets really angry, she can't stop herself going avo-control!
- **CUTE QUOTE:** "I just want to make sure everyone is having a rice time!"
- **SCENT:** Cucumber
- **SERIES:** 2
- **CHARACTER NUMBER:** 2-025
- **BFF:** Cheesy Go-Go (Nom)

Special **EDITION**

I have ◯

Cali Roll

I have ◯

- FLAVORSOME FACT: Cali Roll is as cool as a cucumber and smells like one, too. Despite his name, he never gets crabby. You can tell by looking at him that this Num is all heart.
- CUTE QUOTE: "What's the rush? Like, slow your roll, dude; let's just chill."
- SCENT: Cucumber
- SERIES: 2
- CHARACTER NUMBER: 2-020
- BFF: Veggie Terry (Pizza)

Oni Giri

Special **EDITION**

I have ◯

- FLAVORSOME FACT: Say "hello" or "konnichiwa" to Oni Giri. He never gives his friends a raw deal. This fella succeeds in everything that he does, proving that rice guys can finish first.
- CUTE QUOTE: "I'm always having a ball!"
- SCENT: Ginger
- SERIES: 2
- CHARACTER NUMBER: 2-024
- BFF: Wild Berry Freezie (Freezie Pop)

EggBert Tamago

- 🍮 **FLAVORSOME FACT:** This little Num goes to eggs-traordinary lengths to make his pals giggle. When they crack up, he beats it. He can be a bit stingy, though . . . he's not big on shelling out.
- 🍮 **CUTE QUOTE:** "Don't call me stupid . . . omelette smarter than I look."
- 🍮 **SCENT:** Egg
- 🍮 **SERIES:** 2
- 🍮 **CHARACTER NUMBER:** 2-017
- 🍮 **BFF:** Sunny Omelette (Brunch)

I have ◯

Shin Shiro

- 🍮 **FLAVORSOME FACT:** Shin Shiro is o-fish-ally unique among his Sushi friends. This little guy always dances to his own tuna! He's certainly one of the more musical Num Noms. He loves playing "Chopsticks" on the piano.
- 🍮 **CUTE QUOTE:** "My ginger scent is the root to my happiness!"
- 🍮 **SCENT:** Ginger
- 🍮 **SERIES:** 2
- 🍮 **CHARACTER NUMBER:** 2-026
- 🍮 **BFF:** Ama Ebi (Sushi)

Special **EDITION**

I have ◯

I have ◯

Ama EBi

- **FLAVORSOME FACT:** It pays to carry earplugs if it's band practice night for Ama Ebi. She's a raw-kin drummer with a pair of chopsticks. But sometimes she's a little shellfish and can make a lot of noise doing drum rolls.
- **CUTE QUOTE:** "Got a problem? Just rice above it!"
- **SCENT:** Ginger
- **SERIES:** 2
- **CHARACTER NUMBER:** 2-022
- **BFF:** Shin Shiro (Sushi)

Ina Ree

- **FLAVORSOME FACT:** Ina Ree sure has a fiery personality. If someone fries this Num's nerves, she's bound to lose her tempura with them. That's when you'd batter hope you're not in the firing line!
- **CUTE QUOTE:** "You may think I'm your soy-mate, but I'm not the marine type."
- **SCENT:** Tofu
- **SERIES:** 2
- **CHARACTER NUMBER:** 2-019
- **BFF:** Wasabi Go-Go (Nom)

I have ◯

I have ◯

Phili Roll

- **FLAVORSOME FACT:** Phili has always been a great roll model to her Sushi friends. Others like to follow her lead because she's bento-n success, but she doesn't act like she's the big cheese.
- **CUTE QUOTE:** "Miso happy when I'm just spending time with my girls."
- **SCENT:** Ginger
- **SERIES:** 2
- **CHARACTER NUMBER:** 2-021
- **BFF:** Peppy Roni (Pizza)

Suki Sake

- **FLAVORSOME FACT:** Suki is strong, but he's no meat-head. He looks out for his friends when he's rollin' with his squad. He's cautious, too, and always behaves ginger-ly if they're visiting somewhere new.
- **CUTE QUOTE:** "No need to get cross with me . . . I've got no beef with you!"
- **SCENT:** Ginger
- **SERIES:** 2
- **CHARACTER NUMBER:** 2-023
- **BFF:** B.L.T. (Diner Food)

Special **EDITION**

I have ◯

Veggie Nums

If you carrot all about vegetables, this is what you've bean waiting for! Lettuce begin. . . .

I have ◯

Paula Pumpkin

- 🍠 FLAVORSOME FACT: Paula has carved out her place in the world. She came from the seedy part of town but has squashed any hollow feelings.
- 🍠 CUTE QUOTE: "I am so pumped to see you!"
- 🍠 SCENT: Pumpkin
- 🍠 SERIES: 3
- 🍠 CHARACTER NUMBER: 3-030
- 🍠 BFF: Piney Apple (Fruit)

Bunny Carrot

- 🥕 FLAVORSOME FACT: All the other Num Noms are rooting for this crunchy little hunny. She finds something bunny in any situation!
- 🥕 CUTE QUOTE: "I carrot live without fun and laughter."
- 🥕 SCENT: Carrot
- 🥕 SERIES: 3
- 🥕 CHARACTER NUMBER: 3-028
- 🥕 BFF: Coolie Cucumber (Veggie)

I have ◯

I have ◯

EDa Mama

- FLAVORSOME FACT: Caring Eda is a real Earth mama. She always likes to keep her little ones close to her because she thinks it's important to have inner peas.
- CUTE QUOTE: "Smile, please, every-pody! I just want you all to be hap-pea."
- SCENT: Peas
- SERIES: 3
- CHARACTER NUMBER: 3-027
- BFFS: Pea and Pod Erase-It (Noms)

coolie Cucumber

- FLAVORSOME FACT: Coolie certainly puts the cute into cute-cumber. She's a sight for sore eyes! Her beauty regimen is totally fresh . . . she relaxes by floating the day away in cool water.
- CUTE QUOTE: "Don't follow the same routine every day. Variety is the slice of life."
- SCENT: Cucumber
- SERIES: 3
- CHARACTER NUMBER: 3-032
- BFF: Bunny Carrot (Veggie)

Special EDITION

I have ◯

I have ◯

Emma Eggplant

- **FLAVORSOME FACT:** Veggies . . . will you please mauve aside for the auber-genius, Emma Eggplant? Her cheesy scents of humor makes her a real purple-pleaser.
- **CUTE QUOTE:** "I think I'm really quite eggs-traordinary, don't you?"
- **SCENT:** Eggplant
- **SERIES:** 3
- **CHARACTER NUMBER:** 3-031
- **BFF:** Maya Mallow (Marshmallow)

Carrie Corn

- **FLAVORSOME FACT:** Flower girl Carrie Corn thinks she tells a-maize-ing stories. Unfortunately, most of her pals think they're pretty corny gags.
- **CUTE QUOTE:** "Aw, shucks. I must corn-fess . . . these are the best ears of my life."
- **SCENT:** Sweetcorn
- **SERIES:** 3
- **CHARACTER NUMBER:** 3-029
- **BFF:** Flower Tortilla (Fiesta Food)

I have ◯

Erase-It Noms

These sweet-smelling Noms are unmistakable. But here's the rub . . . you've gotta get your hands on these guys quickly before they disappear!

Nana Erase-It

- **FLAVORSOME FACT:** Nana Erase-It is always up for an adventure. But if she can't get a slice of the action, she splits.
- **CUTE QUOTE:** "When it comes to tunes, I love a musical mash-up."
- **SCENT:** Banana
- **SERIES:** 3
- **CHARACTER NUMBER:** 3-071
- **BFF:** Becky Banana (Fruit)

I have ◯

Slice and Wedge Erase-It

- **FLAVORSOME FACT:** These tangy twins usually rub shoulders just fine. But if Slice ever annoys Wedge, he quickly peels off.
- **CUTE QUOTE:** "Hey, orange you glad we're related?"
- **SCENT:** Orange
- **SERIES:** 3
- **CHARACTER NUMBER:** 3-068
- **BFF:** Oscar Orange (Fruit)

I have ◯

PiP, PUP, and POP Corn Eraser

I have ◯

- **FLAVORSOME FACT:** These little guys are bursting with excitement. Once you've seen them, their mind-popping tricks are impossible to erase from your memory.
- **CUTE QUOTE:** "We don't want to seem puffed-up and corn-ceited, but we really are a-maize-ing."
- **SCENT:** Buttered popcorn
- **SERIES:** 2
- **CHARACTER NUMBER:** 2-117
- **BFFS:** Each other!

Mallow Erase-It

- **FLAVORSOME FACT:** When she wants to mallow out, this li'l softie loves to float in a bowl of milk. You can't catch her when she's the last one in the pool.
- **CUTE QUOTE:** "When I hear a nice remark, it makes me feel all squishy inside."
- **SCENT:** Marshmallow
- **SERIES:** 3
- **CHARACTER NUMBER:** 3-070
- **BFF:** Sara S'mores (Marshmallow)

I have ◯

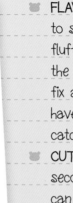

cotton candy Eraser

- **FLAVORSOME FACT:** It's fair to say that this pink and fluffy Nom has her head in the clouds. But she'll always fix any big blunders . . . you'll have to be very quick to catch one of her mistakes.
- **CUTE QUOTE:** "I believe in second chances. What's done can always be undone."
- **SCENT:** Cotton candy
- **SERIES:** 2
- **CHARACTER NUMBER:** 2-116
- **BFF:** Nana Puffs (Fair Food)

I have ◯

Pea anD POD Erase-It

- **FLAVORSOME FACT:** Hush now! Let's have a bit of peas and quiet for these polite Noms. These little guys are never grump-pea, and they always remember to say peas and thank you.
- **CUTE QUOTE:** "We may be small, but we look out for each other in the pod squad."
- **SCENT:** Peas
- **SERIES:** 3
- **CHARACTER NUMBER:** 3-069
- **BFF:** Eda Mama (Veggie)

I have ◯

GLOSS-UP NOMS

Lick your lips and smile.
It's time to greet the Num Noms
who rise and shine every day.

CUCUMBER GLOSS-UP

- 🍬 FLAVORSOME FACT: Don't be salad . . . just give a wink and a smile. This refreshing Nom is way too cool to get herself into a pickle.
- 🍬 CUTE QUOTE: "I'd relish the opportunity to get to know you."
- 🍬 SCENT: Cucumber
- 🍬 SERIES: 2
- 🍬 CHARACTER NUMBER: 2-110
- 🍬 BFF: Mellie Pop (Freezie Pop)

Berry Crème Gloss-UP

- 🍬 FLAVORSOME FACT: Got a problem? Talk to Berry Crème. Other Noms call her the 'Berry Godmother' because she makes everything better.
- 🍬 CUTE QUOTE: "Come on, guys. Why don't you just kiss and make up?"
- 🍬 SCENT: Strawberry
- 🍬 SERIES: 2
- 🍬 CHARACTER NUMBER: 2-129
- 🍬 BFF: B.B. Scoops (Ice Cream)

Special **EDITION**

I have ◯

Peachy Piña Gloss-UP

- **FLAVORSOME FACT:** Savor the twin flavors of this fruity filly. But don't ever make the mistake of double-crossing her. This is one Nom who's not peachy keen about friends with loose lips.
- **CUTE QUOTE:** "Any jokes about me having a split personality are just the pits."
- **SCENTS:** Peach and pineapple
- **SERIES:** 3
- **CHARACTER NUMBER:** 3-079
- **BFF:** Blue Razz Gloss-Up (Nom)

I have ◯

Nilla Gloss-UP

- **FLAVORSOME FACT:** No wonder Nilla Gloss-Up is so popular . . . this versatile Nom can make any treat super-sweet.
- **CUTE QUOTE:** "Read my lips . . . I go great with cherry, strawberry, and chocolate. Oh, and mint. And raspberry. Everything, actually!"
- **SCENT:** Vanilla
- **SERIES:** 1 and 2
- **CHARACTER NUMBERS:** 158 and 2-113
- **BFF:** Van Minty (Ice Cream)

I have ◯

Grapple Gloss-UP

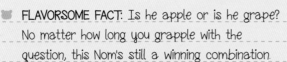

- FLAVORSOME FACT: Is he apple or is he grape? No matter how long you grapple with the question, this Nom's still a winning combination.
- CUTE QUOTE: "My friends always call me out for smacking my lips when I eat"
- SCENTS: Grape and apple
- SERIES: 3
- CHARACTER NUMBER: 3-080
- BFF: Apple Icy (Snow Cone)

I have ◯

Cherry Gloss-UP

- FLAVORSOME FACT: Cherry Gloss-Up is always up-to-date with the latest trends. Naturally she has a soft spot for anything à la mode.
- CUTE QUOTE: "What's my style? Glossy, glam, and never, ever tacky"
- SCENT: Cherry
- SERIES: 1 and 2
- CHARACTER NUMBERS: 164 and 2-115
- BFF: Strawberry Sprinkles (Ice Cream)

 I have ◯

S'mores Gloss-UP

- FLAVORSOME FACT: This little Nom may seem quiet at first. But when she opens up, you'll see there s'more than meets the eye inside.
- CUTE QUOTE: "Mmm . . . I go totally balmy for campfire snacks."
- SCENT: S'mores
- SERIES: 2
- CHARACTER NUMBER: 2-111
- BFF: Mallow Jelly (Jelly Bean)

I have ◯

Berrylicious Gloss-UP

I have ◯

- FLAVORSOME FACT: You might think this sweet-smelling Nom is cold. But that's not the case . . . she just has blue lips. It's berry annoying when she keeps being told to sit by the fire!
- CUTE QUOTE: "C'mon, I am NOT cold. Can we please just gloss over this now?"
- SCENT: Blueberry
- SERIES: 2
- CHARACTER NUMBER: 2-109
- BFF: Berry Froyo (Brunch)

Blue Razz Gloss-UP

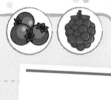

- FLAVORSOME FACT: The other Num Noms know that Blue Razz is a very trustworthy friend. She never spills their secrets . . . her lips are sealed.
- CUTE QUOTE: "Aw, you bought me a lovely bouquet! How did you guess that two-lips are my favorite flowers?"
- SCENTS: Blueberry and raspberry
- SERIES: 3
- CHARACTER NUMBER: 3-081
- BFF: Peachy Piña Gloss-Up (Nom)

I have ◯

I have ◯

? Mr. Icing

🍬 FLAVORSOME FACT: All that glitters is not gold . . . but sometimes it's a golden Gloss-Up Nom! Mr. Icing has a twinkle in his eye, but if Mrs. Icing talks too much, you can see him glazing over.

🍬 CUTE QUOTE: "Life is truly golden when you cover yourself in love."

🍬 SCENT: Mystery

🍬 SERIES: 2

🍬 CHARACTER NUMBER: 2-135

🍬 BFF: Mrs. Icing (Cupcake)

MintBerry Gloss-UP

🍬 FLAVORSOME FACT: Marvelous Mintberry Gloss-Up doesn't put up with people who get fresh with her. No matter how much her friends pout, this feisty Nom never takes lip from anyone.

🍬 CUTE QUOTE: "If they get lippy with me, I just give 'em a mouthful."

🍬 SCENTS: Blueberry and mint

🍬 SERIES: 3

🍬 CHARACTER NUMBER: 3-076

🍬 BFF: B. Berry Mallow (Marshmallow)

I have ◯

BuBBly Gloss-UP

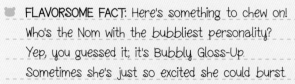

- FLAVORSOME FACT: Here's something to chew on! Who's the Nom with the bubbliest personality? Yep, you guessed it; it's Bubbly Gloss-Up. Sometimes she's just so excited she could burst.
- CUTE QUOTE: "Pucker up and blow me a kiss!"
- SCENT: Bubblegum
- SERIES: 2
- CHARACTER NUMBER: 2-108
- BFF: Bubbly Jelly (Jelly Bean)

I have ◯

Cotton Crème Gloss-UP

- FLAVORSOME FACT: With two pretty colors, some say that this special Nom is spoiled cotton. But when questioned, she remains tight-lipped.
- CUTE QUOTE: "Is it my fault that I'm just so lip-smackingly good to look at?"
- SCENT: Cotton candy
- SERIES: 2
- CHARACTER NUMBER: 2-132
- BFF: Twinzy Puffs (Fair Food)

Special **EDITION**

I have ◯

Orange Piña Gloss-UP

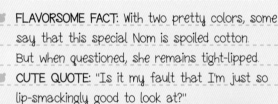

- FLAVORSOME FACT: Orange Piña Gloss-Up always keeps a stiff upper lip. But her totally tropical flavors usually shine through in the end.
- CUTE QUOTE: "My tangy sweetness is so refreshing on balmy days."
- SCENT: Orange and pineapple
- SERIES: 3
- CHARACTER NUMBER: 3-073
- BFF: Tina Tangerine (Candy)

I have ◯

Nana Gloss-UP

- **FLAVORSOME FACT:** This sweet-natured Nom is balmy about her BFF. In fact, she loves her so much that it's hard to peel them away from each other.
- **CUTE QUOTE:** "I can't imagine being without my BFF. She is my salve-ation."
- **SCENT:** Banana
- **SERIES:** 1
- **CHARACTER NUMBER:** 159
- **BFF:** Berry Berry Swirl (Cupcake)

I have ◯

Mint Crème Gloss-UP

Special **EDITION**

- **FLAVORSOME FACT:** Fresh-faced Mint Crème Gloss-Up is really something special. She's the crème de la crème of the Num Noms. Why would you chew-se another?
- **CUTE QUOTE:** "A Gloss-Up get-together? I can hardly contain my excite-mint."
- **SCENT:** Mint
- **SERIES:** 2
- **CHARACTER NUMBER:** 2-128
- **BFF:** Mint T. Cream (Ice Cream)

I have ◯

Van-Berry Gloss-Up

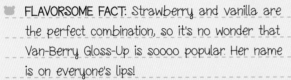

- **FLAVORSOME FACT:** Strawberry and vanilla are the perfect combination, so it's no wonder that Van-Berry Gloss-Up is soooo popular. Her name is on everyone's lips!
- **CUTE QUOTE:** "Aw, you guys make me shine."
- **SCENTS:** Strawberry and vanilla
- **SERIES:** 3
- **CHARACTER NUMBER:** 3-078
- **BFF:** Sophia Strawberry (Donut)

I have ◯

Cola Gloss-Up

- **FLAVORSOME FACT:** You'll usually find this Nom fizzin' around the kitchen. Her scrumptious cooking is bound to get your lips tingling.
- **CUTE QUOTE:** "I always try to add some sparkle to my day."
- **SCENT:** Cola soda
- **SERIES:** 2
- **CHARACTER NUMBER:** 2-112
- **BFF:** Cherry Scoop (Ice Cream)

I have ◯

Orange Gloss-Up

- **FLAVORSOME FACT:** Orange Gloss-Up is a burst of energy. Wherever she goes, she brings zip and zest, and you'll soon hear peels of laughter.
- **CUTE QUOTE:** "I like to give everyone their juice desserts."
- **SCENT:** Orange
- **SERIES:** 1
- **CHARACTER NUMBER:** 161
- **BFF:** Sherry Berry (Ice Cream)

I have ◯

I have ◯

Nana Crème Gloss-UP

- **FLAVORSOME FACT:** Followers of fashion will already know about this stylish Nom. Scrumptious Nana Crème is a real glamour puss. With her sleek and polished looks, she's the crème of the crop.
- **CUTE QUOTE:** "I keep my eyes peeled for special offers on makeup."
- **SCENT:** Banana
- **SERIES:** 2
- **CHARACTER NUMBER:** 2-130
- **BFF:** Nea Pop (Freezie Pop)

Choco-Razz Gloss-UP

- **FLAVORSOME FACT:** This talented Nom loves all the razzle-dazzle of the music biz. Choco-Razz is super-slick in the spotlight, and when she rocks out, she always curls her lip.
- **CUTE QUOTE:** "My gigs are choc-full of berry good tunes."
- **SCENTS:** Chocolate and raspberry
- **SERIES:** 3
- **CHARACTER NUMBER:** 3-077
- **BFF:** Rachel Raspberry (Marshmallow)

I have ◯

Mintee Gloss-UP

- FLAVORSOME FACT: Merry Mintee is like a breath of fresh air wherever she goes. You can't help being won over by her compli-mints.
- CUTE QUOTE: "It's important to be up fresh and early each day."
- SCENT: Mint
- SERIES: 1
- CHARACTER NUMBER: 165
- BFF: Betsy Bubblegum (Cupcake)

I have ◯

Straw-Nana Gloss-UP

- FLAVORSOME FACT: Straw-Nana is the Gloss-Up who loves to gossip. But although she gets all the juicy details on the other Num Noms, she knows when to zip her lip.
- CUTE QUOTE: "Excuse me. I may be clutching at strawberries here, but do I know you from somewhere?"
- SCENTS: Strawberry and banana
- SERIES: 3
- CHARACTER NUMBER: 3-074
- BFF: Sugar Nana (Marshmallow)

I have ◯

Candy Crème Gloss-UP

🟣 **FLAVORSOME FACT:** If you tell this glossy girl that her head is in the pink, fluffy clouds, she'll laugh till she's blue in the face.

🟣 **CUTE QUOTE:** "I love straws, because they certainly come in candy."

🟣 **SCENT:** Cotton candy

🟣 **SERIES:** 2

🟣 **CHARACTER NUMBER:** 2-131

🟣 **BFF:** Cotton Jelly (Jelly Bean)

Special **EDITION**

I have ◯

Choco S'mores Gloss-UP

🟣 **FLAVORSOME FACT:** Chatty Choco S'mores has the gift of the gab. But if she doesn't like what you're saying, she tells you to button your lip.

🟣 **CUTE QUOTE:** "You want s'more chocolate? You can never have too much!"

🟣 **SCENTS:** S'mores and chocolate

🟣 **SERIES:** 3

🟣 **CHARACTER NUMBER:** 3-082

🟣 **BFF:** Cocoa Mallow (Marshmallow)

I have ◯

Peachy Gloss-UP

🟣 **FLAVORSOME FACT:** This girly Gloss-Up isn't the pits; she's a real peach. Her sweet-smelling, fruity flavor is lip-smackingly lovely.

🟣 **CUTE QUOTE:** "I work very hard to keep my 'peaches and cream' complexion."

🟣 **SCENT:** Peach

🟣 **SERIES:** 1

🟣 **CHARACTER NUMBER:** 162

🟣 **BFF:** Patty Peach (Cupcake)

I have ◯

Glitter Surprise Gloss-UP

- **FLAVORSOME FACT:** You never know what you're going to get with Glitter Surprise. But one thing's for sure; this mysterious Nom will definitely bring some glitz and glamour into your life.
- **CUTE QUOTE:** "Shhh ... I will tell you what my secret is; I can read lips."
- **SCENT:** Mystery
- **SERIES:** 3
- **CHARACTER NUMBER:** 3-083
- **BFF:** Swirls Lolly (Candy)

I have ◯

Piña Gloss-UP

- **FLAVORSOME FACT:** Don't be fooled by appearances. Piña's salving grace is that her prickly exterior hides her exotic flavors. She can run rings around her friends!
- **CUTE QUOTE:** "You probably won't guess just by looking at me ... but inside I'm all super-sweetness."
- **SCENT:** Pineapple
- **SERIES:** 1
- **CHARACTER NUMBER:** 160
- **BFF:** Lisa Lemon (Ice Cream)

I have ◯

Cucumber Melon Gloss-Up

I have ◯

- **FLAVORSOME FACT:** When Cucumber Melon is upset, she bites her lip and doesn't say anything. This sensitive Nom would hate to water up in front of everyone.
- **CUTE QUOTE:** "Please give me a moment . . . I'm trying to keep my cool."
- **SCENTS:** Cucumber and watermelon
- **SERIES:** 3
- **CHARACTER NUMBER:** 3-075
- **BFF:** Sparkle Mellie (Candy)

Nilla Crème Gloss-Up

Special **EDITION**

- **FLAVORSOME FACT:** Eager Nilla Crème just loves to whip up excitement by creating creamy desserts. However, she often glosses over her role in making a mess.
- **CUTE QUOTE:** "It's impossible to get angry with me. Vanilla is flavor of the month all year round!"
- **SCENT:** Vanilla
- **SERIES:** 2
- **CHARACTER NUMBER:** 2-133
- **BFF:** Mara Schino (Cupcake)

I have ◯

Cherry Vanilla Gloss-UP

- **FLAVORSOME FACT:** This li'l fella turns red in the face when he gets angry. But he means what he says. He never pays you lip service.
- **CUTE QUOTE:** "I'm not the most polished Num Nom, but I'm cherry nice, really."
- **SCENTS:** Cherry and vanilla
- **SERIES:** 3
- **CHARACTER NUMBER:** 3-072
- **BFF:** Chloe Cola (Snow Cone)

I have ◯

Berry Gloss-UP

- **FLAVORSOME FACT:** Berry Gloss-Up doesn't enjoy being the center of attention. But she always keeps her cool if she gets in a jam!
- **CUTE QUOTE:** "Making jokes about me is just the last straw-berry."
- **SCENT:** Strawberry
- **SERIES:** 1 and 2
- **CHARACTER NUMBERS:** 163 and 2-114
- **BFF:** Choco Berry (Cupcake)

I have ◯

Cotton Candy Gloss-UP

- **FLAVORSOME FACT:** Always bright and breezy, Cotton Candy Gloss-Up is one sweet little lady. Her light and airy personality is a real treat.
- **CUTE QUOTE:** "I just love giving out candy kisses . . . mwaaah!"
- **SCENT:** Cotton candy
- **SERIES:** 2
- **CHARACTER NUMBER:** 2-107
- **BFF:** Sugar Puffs (Fair Food)

I have ◯

GO-GO NOMS

Introducing the super-speedy motorized Num Noms.
These guys are always going fast, so you'll
have to grab them while you can!

I have ◯

Cherry Jelly Go-Go

- 🐻 FLAVORSOME FACT: Cherry Jelly's friends call her "the peacemaker." That's because when things get sticky, she calms everyone down.
- 🐻 CUTE QUOTE: "Sometimes it pays to make quick decisions."
- 🐻 SCENT: Cherry
- 🐻 SERIES: 2
- 🐻 CHARACTER NUMBER: 2-093
- 🐻 BFF: Cherry Cheesecake (Cupcake)

Tropical Go-Go

- 🐻 FLAVORSOME FACT: Anyone seen Tropical Go-Go? With her exotic flavors, search places with plenty of sand, sun, and smoothies!
- 🐻 CUTE QUOTE: "I leave no stone unturned when I'm looking for fun."
- 🐻 SCENT: Mango
- 🐻 SERIES: 1
- 🐻 CHARACTER NUMBER: 149
- 🐻 BFF: Lemony Burst (Cupcake)

I have ◯

Jammin' Razzy Go-Go

I have ○

- 🐻 FLAVORSOME FACT: Talented Jammin' Razzy dazzles everyone with her funky moves on the dance floor. So much so that she's now the toast of the town!
- 🐻 CUTE QUOTE: "Success wasn't just handed to me on a plate. So I try to preserve what I've got!"
- 🐻 SCENT: Raspberry
- 🐻 SERIES: 2
- 🐻 CHARACTER NUMBER: 2-095
- 🐻 BFF: Willy Waffles (Brunch)

Ketchup Go-Go

- 🐻 FLAVORSOME FACT: When you first meet her, you'll think this saucy Nom is a little dippy. But she's really dependable and loves to ketchup with friends at her book club. She's very well red!
- 🐻 CUTE QUOTE: "I'm a big bottle of happiness!"
- 🐻 SCENT: Ketchup
- 🐻 SERIES: 2
- 🐻 CHARACTER NUMBER: 2-100
- 🐻 BFF: Frenchie Fries (Diner Food)

I have ○

ChoCo Go-Go

- **FLAVORSOME FACT:** This little Nom has a big problem . . . she's a chocoholic. For her, a little too much chocolate is just about right
- **CUTE QUOTE:** "You think you've got it tough? Nobody knows the truffles I've seen"
- **SCENT:** Chocolate
- **SERIES:** 1
- **CHARACTER NUMBER:** 155
- **BFF:** Nilla Twirl (Ice Cream)

I have ◯

Icy Berry Go-Go

- **FLAVORSOME FACT:** Life is always frantic for Icy Berry Go-Go, so she's always whizzing around. But no matter how busy she gets, she always remains totally chill
- **CUTE QUOTE:** "I talk until I'm blue in the face"
- **SCENT:** Blue raspberry
- **SERIES:** 2
- **CHARACTER NUMBER:** 2-091
- **BFF:** Cassie Cola (Diner Food)

I have ◯

Butterscotch Go-Go

- **FLAVORSOME FACT:** This sweet-flavored Nom tries to make a good impression. She believes in pudding her best foot forward.
- **CUTE QUOTE:** "You can't be too soft on people. You gotta give 'em toffee love"
- **SCENT:** Caramel
- **SERIES:** 2
- **CHARACTER NUMBER:** 2-098
- **BFF:** Raspberry Jelly (Jelly Bean)

I have ◯

Banana Go-Go

- **FLAVORSOME FACT:** Good luck if you're trying to find Banana Go-Go. If you do see her, she'll be zooming off. She knows when to split....
- **CUTE QUOTE:** "There's nothing like letting loose, spinning around and around, and going totally bananas!"
- **SCENT:** Banana
- **SERIES:** 1
- **CHARACTER NUMBER:** 147
- **BFF:** Tango Mango (Ice Cream)

I have ◯

Pickly Go-Go

- **FLAVORSOME FACT:** This tough guy's wheels can be a bit cumber-some at times. But if he gets himself in a pickle, this Nom doesn't make a big dill out of it.
- **CUTE QUOTE:** "Next time you wanna play a card game, make sure you dill me in."
- **SCENT:** Pickle
- **SERIES:** 2
- **CHARACTER NUMBER:** 2-103
- **BFF:** Sara Strawberry (Ice Cream)

I have ◯

Icy Peach Go-Go

- FLAVORSOME FACT: Got something on your mind? This little gal gives great advice. Her friends respect her because she always practices what she peaches. Way to go-go, Icy Peach!
- CUTE QUOTE: "You give me a warm, fuzzy feeling inside."
- SCENT: Peach
- SERIES: 2
- CHARACTER NUMBER: 2-090
- BFF: Parker Peach (Ice Cream)

I have ◯

Mintee Go-Go

- FLAVORSOME FACT: The cold is where Mintee Go-Go loves to be. On a hot day, you might find her in the freezer cuddling with the ice cubes. Well, she can be a little fresh at times.
- CUTE QUOTE: "You look thirsty. Would you care for some refresh-mints?"
- SCENT: Mint
- SERIES: 1
- CHARACTER NUMBER: 153
- BFF: Choco Nana (Cupcake)

I have ◯

Buttery Go-Go

- **FLAVORSOME FACT:** Busy Buttery Go-Go is a bit of a control freak. Whatever project he's working on, there's no margarine for error. He also tends to spread himself way too thin.
- **CUTE QUOTE:** "It was due yesterday? Butter late than never; that's my motto."
- **SCENT:** Butter
- **SERIES:** 2
- **CHARACTER NUMBER:** 2-097
- **BFF:** Maple Cakes (Brunch)

I have ◯

Glittery Berry Go-Go

Special **EDITION**

- **FLAVORSOME FACT:** Prepare to meet the glitziest Go-Go on the block. Glittery Berry's sparkling sense of humor is a berry big hit among the glitter-raspberries.
- **CUTE QUOTE:** "All of my friends say I have a twinkle in my eye."
- **SCENT:** Raspberry
- **SERIES:** 2
- **CHARACTER NUMBER:** 2-106
- **BFF:** Strawberry Cream (Cupcake)

I have ◯

Mango Jelly Go-Go

- FLAVORSOME FACT: Ditzy Mango Jelly Go-Go has come unstuck on quite a few occasions. She has a naughty habit of trying to make people jelly-ous.
- CUTE QUOTE: "Does anyone want to be my dancing partner? After all, it takes two to mango!"
- SCENT: Mango
- SERIES: 2
- CHARACTER NUMBER: 2-092
- BFF: Kiwi Freezie (Freezie Pop)

I have ◯

Nilla Go-Go

- FLAVORSOME FACT: Nilla could be the fastest Go-Go around. You might glimpse this super-speedy Nom as she whooshes by. Get your skates on if you want to say hi!
- CUTE QUOTE: "My special flavor? Why, it's the essence of good taste."
- SCENT: Vanilla
- SERIES: 1
- CHARACTER NUMBER: 157
- BFF: Orange Cream (Ice Cream)

Special **EDITION**

I have ◯

RazzBerry Go-Go

- **FLAVORSOME FACT:** It's time for a little razzmatazz! And here's the perfect Nom for the job, Ms. Razzberry Go-Go. She's full of pizzazz!
- **CUTE QUOTE:** "I can be a bit of a razz-cal when I get go-going"
- **SCENT:** Raspberry
- **SERIES:** 1
- **CHARACTER NUMBER:** 152
- **BFF:** Cherry Chip (Ice Cream)

I have ◯

Lemony Go-Go

- **FLAVORSOME FACT:** The other Num Noms admire Lemony for her positive outlook. She's got tons of energy and plenty of get-up-and-go-go.
- **CUTE QUOTE:** "I'm no sourpuss . . . my smile is my best feature"
- **SCENT:** Lemon
- **SERIES:** 1
- **CHARACTER NUMBER:** 148
- **BFF:** Sweetie Strawberry (Cupcake)

I have ◯

Icy Piña Go-Go

- **FLAVORSOME FACT:** Despite her appearance, Icy Piña's not square at all. In a race, she can run pineapple rings around all the other Go-Gos!
- **CUTE QUOTE:** "If people accuse me of being square, I feel crushed"
- **SCENT:** Pineapple
- **SERIES:** 2
- **CHARACTER NUMBER:** 2-089
- **BFF:** M. Mallow (Cupcake)

I have ◯

I have ◯

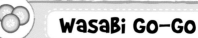

WasaBi Go-Go

- **FLAVORSOME FACT:** Say 'wassup' to Wasabi Go-Go, if you dare. But be warned; this mini martial arts master has a real kick. His carroty chop leaves others green with envy.
- **CUTE QUOTE:** "Come on, hot stuff! You can't call yourself a Go-Go at that speed. Let's get moving. Chop-chop!"
- **SCENT:** Cucumber
- **SERIES:** 2
- **CHARACTER NUMBER:** 2-104
- **BFF:** Ina Ree (Sushi)

Jammin' Berry Go-Go

- **FLAVORSOME FACT:** This Nom likes to take it easy while listening to her reggae tunes. But when she's jammin', she goes wild.
- **CUTE QUOTE:** "I'd love to spread my wings and listen to reggae in the West Indies. If P.B.N.J. was interested, I'd Jamaica come, too!"
- **SCENT:** Wildberry
- **SERIES:** 2
- **CHARACTER NUMBER:** 2-096
- **BFF:** P.B.N.J. (Diner Food)

I have ◯

Cheesy Go-Go

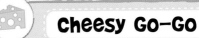

- **FLAVORSOME FACT:** This smart and savory Go-Go can brie a little full of herself. Although she's really a softie, she sometimes acts like the big cheese and behaves like no one is Gouda-nough for her.
- **CUTE QUOTE:** "Your argument has more holes in it than Swiss cheese!"
- **SCENT:** Cheese
- **SERIES:** 2
- **CHARACTER NUMBER:** 2-101
- **BFF:** Ami Avocado (Sushi)

I have ◯

BUBBly Go-Go

- **FLAVORSOME FACT:** This happy-go-go-lucky Nom is no bubble-head. It's true that she always seems to get herself into sticky situations, but she's clever enough to pop free.
- **CUTE QUOTE:** "When you're feeling in the pink, why not give the world a wink?"
- **SCENT:** Bubblegum
- **SERIES:** 1
- **CHARACTER NUMBER:** 156
- **BFF:** Betty B-Day (Cupcake)

Special EDITION

I have ◯

Cherry Go-Go

- 🐻 FLAVORSOME FACT: All the other Num Noms think that Cherry is a real go-go-getter with a bright future. With her cherryful attitude, she'll get what she wants . . . easy as cherry pie.
- 🐻 CUTE QUOTE: "I'm a cheery cherry!"
- 🐻 SCENT: Cherry
- 🐻 SERIES: 1
- 🐻 CHARACTER NUMBER: 151
- 🐻 BFF: Nilla Cream (Cupcake)

I have ◯

Peanut Go-Go

- 🐻 FLAVORSOME FACT: Peanut Go-Go walnut fail to impress you with her acrobatic skills. She loves the circus and is totally nuts about elephants.
- 🐻 CUTE QUOTE: "I've gotta be the only Num Nom who will work for peanuts."
- 🐻 SCENT: Circus peanut
- 🐻 SERIES: 2
- 🐻 CHARACTER NUMBER: 2-099
- 🐻 BFF: Nana Splits (Ice Cream)

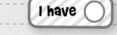
I have ◯

Caramelly Go-Go

- 🐻 FLAVORSOME FACT: Wow, this little Go-Go can move at quite a lick. But you'd better watch out if you bump into her . . . some days she's super-sweet and other days she's salty.
- 🐻 CUTE QUOTE: "Check these silky-smooth moves!"
- 🐻 SCENT: Caramel
- 🐻 SERIES: 1
- 🐻 CHARACTER NUMBER: 154
- 🐻 BFF: Choco Nilla (Ice Cream)

I have ◯

Chili Go-Go

- **FLAVORSOME FACT:** Keep your distance! This mean machine is feared by all for his fiery personality. He has a hot temper, even though he's just a little chili.
- **CUTE QUOTE:** "I didn't mean to make you cry. I just can't help it if everyone gets overheated around me."
- **SCENT:** Chili
- **SERIES:** 2
- **CHARACTER NUMBER:** 2-102
- **BFF:** Tropi-Cali Pop (Freezie Pop)

I have ◯

StrawBerry Go-Go

- **FLAVORSOME FACT:** There is a buzz about Strawberry. She has been known to shake with excitement before her friends come over to play.
- **CUTE QUOTE:** "Have you seen the price of milkshakes lately? It's daylight st-robbery."
- **SCENT:** Strawberry
- **SERIES:** 1
- **CHARACTER NUMBER:** 150
- **BFF:** Choco Cream (Ice Cream)

I have ◯

Grape Jelly Go-Go

- **FLAVORSOME FACT:** This gorgeous Go-Go is grape company to have around. That's because she spreads love and sweetness wherever she goes.
- **CUTE QUOTE:** "You won't catch me complaining. I've no raisin to wine about what I hear through the grapevine"
- **SCENT:** Grape
- **SERIES:** 2
- **CHARACTER NUMBER:** 2-094
- **BFF:** C.H.Z. (Diner Food)

I have ◯

GingerBread Go-Go

- **FLAVORSOME FACT:** Gifted Gingerbread Go-Go has a special talent; this clever Nom is a wonderful designer. When it comes to decorating, she really shines and her houses always look sweet!
- **CUTE QUOTE:** "I believe you should sparkle all year round, not just during the holidays."
- **SCENT:** Gingerbread
- **SERIES:** 2
- **CHARACTER NUMBER:** 2-105
- **BFF:** Sugar Berry (Cupcake)

Special **EDITION**

I have ◯

Light-Up Noms

Let's put the spotlight on these shining stars.
With their lovely lights, they are sure
to brighten everyone's day.

Grape Light-Up

- FLAVORSOME FACT: Despite what others might say, Grape Light-Up isn't too sour. This adorable Nom is actually all sweetness and light.
- CUTE QUOTE: "I've got a secret ... I'm filled with a di-vine light."
- SCENT: Grape
- SERIES: Lights 1
- CHARACTER NUMBER: L-038
- BFF: Grape Gummy (Gummy)

I have ◯

BlueBerry Light-Up

- FLAVORSOME FACT: Energetic Blueberry Light-Up works berry hard from first light. It's not surprising that at bedtime, she's out like a light!
- CUTE QUOTE: "My achievements always make me glow with pride."
- SCENT: Blueberry
- SERIES: Lights 1
- CHARACTER NUMBER: L-034
- BFF: Glitter Berry (Gummy)

I have ◯

I have ◯

BuBBly Light-UP

- FLAVORSOME FACT: This charming little Nom is so lighthearted that she literally floats through life. Whenever she blows into town, everyone's eyes light up.
- CUTE QUOTE: "Can I help you out? I just want to lighten your load!"
- SCENT: Bubblegum
- SERIES: Lights 1
- CHARACTER NUMBER: L-039
- BFF: Bubblegum Slushy (Snow Cone)

Orange Light-UP

- FLAVORSOME FACT: Early riser Orange Light-Up is always the first Num Nom to see the light of day. It's amazing how much zest she has first thing in the morning.
- CUTE QUOTE: "C'mon, everyone! It's 6:00 AM. Wakey, wakey . . . rise and shine!"
- SCENT: Orange
- SERIES: Lights 1
- CHARACTER NUMBER: L-035
- BFF: Orange Freezie (Freezie Pop)

I have ◯

146

Berry Light-UP

- **FLAVORSOME FACT:** All the other Num Noms talk to Berry Light-Up when they want some advice. It's easy to see why ..... her illuminating words of wisdom help them see things in a new light.
- **CUTE QUOTE:** "I can solve a problem faster than the seed of light"
- **SCENT:** Strawberry
- **SERIES:** Lights 1
- **CHARACTER NUMBER:** L-032
- **BFF:** Nea Snow (Snow Cone)

I have ◯

Mintee Light-UP

- **FLAVORSOME FACT:** Is that a light coming from the kitchen? Yep, it's Mintee Light-Up cooking up some tasty treats. With her knowledge of herbs, she can throw light on many mystery recipes.
- **CUTE QUOTE:** "I like to experi-mint with light meals and snacks."
- **SCENT:** Mint
- **SERIES:** Lights 1
- **CHARACTER NUMBER:** L-040
- **BFF:** Bubble Gummy (Gummy)

I have ◯

RaspBerry Light-UP

- 🐻 FLAVORSOME FACT: When she's not blowing raspberries, this perky Nom loves to amuse her friends with funny jokes. She says that there's nothing quite like it for lightening the mood.
- 🐻 CUTE QUOTE: "When I think about lightbulbs, they always give me a bright idea!"
- 🐻 SCENT: Raspberry
- 🐻 SERIES: Lights 1
- 🐻 CHARACTER NUMBER: L-036
- 🐻 BFF: Raz Sugar (Gummy)

I have ◯

Kiwi Light-UP

- 🐻 FLAVORSOME FACT: When the Light-Up Noms want a new adventure, they have to check with Kiwi before they go. Luckily, she always gives them the green light.
- 🐻 CUTE QUOTE: "I love to explore the countryside. It's no surprise I'm the greenest Light-Up Nom!"
- 🐻 SCENT: Kiwi
- 🐻 SERIES: Lights 1
- 🐻 CHARACTER NUMBER: L-033
- 🐻 BFF: Piña Gummy (Gummy)

I have ◯

Cherry Light-UP

- **FLAVORSOME FACT:** It's time to shine a light on delectable Ms. Cherry Light-Up. She's such a great friend to the other Num Noms. She really lights up their lives.
- **CUTE QUOTE:** "Cut it out or you'll make me turn red. . . . I'm really glowing now!"
- **SCENT:** Cherry
- **SERIES:** Lights 1
- **CHARACTER NUMBER:** L-031
- **BFF:** Cherry Freezie (Freezie Pop)

I have ◯

Peachy Light-UP

- **FLAVORSOME FACT:** This flashy Nom loves the bright lights of the city. Whether she's dancing in the disco lights or playing sports in the floodlights, she's always de-light-ful company.
- **CUTE QUOTE:** "Don't be sad . . . there's always light at the end of the tunnel."
- **SCENT:** Peach
- **SERIES:** Lights 1
- **CHARACTER NUMBER:** L-037
- **BFF:** Peachy Icy (Snow Cone)

I have ◯

Stamp-It Noms

Why not add these cute little Stamp-Its to your collection? They leave a lasting impression wherever they go!

I have ◯

Berry Gummy Stamp-It

- 🍬 FLAVORSOME FACT: Berry Gummy never stops talking. She just keeps flapping her gums for hours!
- 🍬 CUTE QUOTE: "I will keep saying this until I'm blue in the face ... I am NOT a chatterbox"
- 🍬 SCENT: Blueberry
- 🍬 SERIES: 3
- 🍬 CHARACTER NUMBER: 3-085
- 🍬 BFF: Lily Lemony (Candy)

Peachy Stamp-It

- 🍬 FLAVORSOME FACT: This li'l Nom is always talking about her plans, but most of her ideas are pie in the sky!
- 🍬 CUTE QUOTE: "You've just got to peach for the stars if you want to be a success!"
- 🍬 SCENT: Peach
- 🍬 SERIES: 3
- 🍬 CHARACTER NUMBER: 3-089
- 🍬 BFF: Georgia Peach (Fruit)

Special **EDITION**

I have ◯

Lemon Gummy Stamp-It

- **FLAVORSOME FACT:** For Lemon Gummy, home is where the heart is. This humble Nom loves her family and is a sucker for visiting her old stamping grounds.
- **CUTE QUOTE:** "My mom always told me that the lemon never falls far from the tree."
- **SCENT:** Lemon
- **SERIES:** 2
- **CHARACTER NUMBER:** 2-082
- **BFF:** Tori Toro (Sushi)

I have ◯

caramel Stamp-It

Special **EDITION**

- **FLAVORSOME FACT:** This talented artist loves to put her unique stamp on her work. Her originals sell for megabucks, but she will make prints for free.
- **CUTE QUOTE:** "I can't help being a success! At art shows, my pictures stamp out all the competition."
- **SCENT:** Caramel apple
- **SERIES:** 2
- **CHARACTER NUMBER:** 2-088
- **BFF:** Annie Apple (Fair Food)

I have ◯

B-Day Gummy Stamp-It

- 🐾 FLAVORSOME FACT: When it's time to celebrate, B-Day Gummy wants to impress her friends by throwing a big party. Her parties are so popular, her guests stamp-ede to get there.
- 🐾 CUTE QUOTE: "I print my own party invitations."
- 🐾 SCENT: Birthday cake
- 🐾 SERIES: 2
- 🐾 CHARACTER NUMBER: 2-083
- 🐾 BFF: Nilla Froyo (Brunch)

I have ◯

Donut Stamp-It

- 🐾 FLAVORSOME FACT: Soft-hearted and super-sweet, little Donut Stamp-It fills the hole in all her friends' hearts.
- 🐾 CUTE QUOTE: "Whaddya mean, 'do-nut stamp it'? That's who I am. That's what I do!"
- 🐾 SCENT: Donut
- 🐾 SERIES: 3
- 🐾 CHARACTER NUMBER: 3-084
- 🐾 BFF: Maple Sugars (Donut)

I have ◯

Cherry Gummy Stamp-It

- 🐾 FLAVORSOME FACT: Cherry Gummy can get a little hot under the collar. She has fire in her heart and you just can't stamp it out.
- 🐾 CUTE QUOTE: "Come on, guys, let's print the town red. It'll be cherry good fun."
- 🐾 SCENT: Cherry
- 🐾 SERIES: 2
- 🐾 CHARACTER NUMBER: 2-085
- 🐾 BFF: Berry Twirl (Ice Cream)

I have ◯

BlueBerry StamP–It

- **FLAVORSOME FACT:** No-nonsense Blueberry Stamp-It is famous among the Num Noms for driving a hard bargain. That's because for her, it's all or muffin.
- **CUTE QUOTE:** "Hey, I don't just rubber-stamp any old deal, you know."
- **SCENT:** Blueberry
- **SERIES:** 3
- **CHARACTER NUMBER:** 3-088
- **BFF:** Triple Berry Icy (Snow Cone)

I have ◯

Mint Gummy StamP–It

- **FLAVORSOME FACT:** She had a few sticky moments when she was starting out, but it was obvious early on that hardworking Mint Gummy would put her stamp on the world. It was just mint to be.
- **CUTE QUOTE:** "Word of advice . . . you only get one chance to make a first impression."
- **SCENT:** Mint
- **SERIES:** 2
- **CHARACTER NUMBER:** 2-087
- **BFF:** Mint Berry (Cupcake)

I have ◯

Berry Stamp-It

- **FLAVORSOME FACT:** Here's one little fruity cutie that's definitely worth adding to your collection. You wouldn't be drawing the last straw with this Nom . . . she really is berry valuable and ready to make her mark on the world.
- **CUTE QUOTE:** "Take a look at my small print . . ."
- **SCENT:** Strawberry
- **SERIES:** 3
- **CHARACTER NUMBER:** 3-087
- **BFF:** Razzi Berry (Donut)

I have ◯

Candy Gummy Stamp-It

- **FLAVORSOME FACT:** Joyful Candy Gummy enjoys all the fun at the fair. She loves to go on fairground rides, especially ones where she's spun up in the air. If she has to run outside, she always gets a stamp so that she can come back in!
- **CUTE QUOTE:** "I love stampin' in time to the fairground tunes."
- **SCENT:** Cotton candy
- **SERIES:** 2
- **CHARACTER NUMBER:** 2-084
- **BFF:** Berry Puffs (Fair Food)

I have ◯

Melon Gummy Stamp-It

- **FLAVORSOME FACT:** This clever Nom can multitask . . . she chews gum and walks at the same time. But she is a bit spoiled. If she doesn't get her own way, she sulks, stamps around, and has a stamper tantrum.
- **CUTE QUOTE:** "Who wants to be a melon-naire? I do!"
- **SCENT:** Watermelon
- **SERIES:** 3
- **CHARACTER NUMBER:** 3-086
- **BFF:** Mia Mango (Candy)

I have ◯

Wild Berry Gummy Stamp-It

- **FLAVORSOME FACT:** All the other Stamp-It Noms look up to Wild Berry Gummy and come to her with their ideas. It's berry important to get her stamp of approval.
- **CUTE QUOTE:** "We all go a bit wild sometimes, but I believe in stamping out really bad behavior."
- **SCENT:** Wildberry
- **SERIES:** 2
- **CHARACTER NUMBER:** 2-086
- **BFF:** Berry Waffles (Brunch)

I have ◯

InDex

Trying to find a favorite Num Nom? They're all listed here, along with the page number each one appears on.

POP STOP

Did you find Pip, Pup, and Pop Corn Erasers hiding with the Nums? They're on pages 32, 51, and 93.